ROCK BOTTOM

An Imogene Museum Mystery

Book 1

JERUSHA JONES

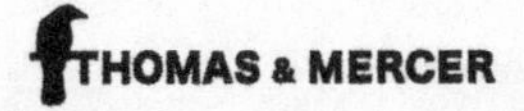

This is a work of fiction. Names, characters, organizations, places, events, and incidents are either products of the author's imagination or are used fictitiously.

Published by Thomas & Mercer, Seattle
www.apub.com

ISBN-13: 9781477829202
ISBN-10: 1477829202

Cover design by Elizabeth Berry MacKenney

Printed in the United States of America

CHAPTER 1

I wandered around the Imogene Museum's ballroom, checking exhibits. They tend to stay where they're put, but you never know.

"You're prowling, Meredith," Lindsay Smith called from the gift shop in what used to be the ladies' cloakroom.

Like everything else about the museum, the cloakroom is generous, built on a scale to accommodate the glamorous furs and silk wraps of fashionable visitors who came from as far away as Portland, Seattle, and sometimes Washington, DC, for party weekends before the First World War. Now the room makes an excellent welcome center and gift shop just off the old mansion's main entrance.

"Killing time," I replied.

"I can't believe you promised Greg you'd wait until he got here. That must be killing *you*."

Greg Boykin, my graduate student intern from Oregon State University, was due to arrive in about an hour, give or take the amount of traffic he had to forge through on I-205 during the evening commute.

"It'll be worth it to see his face when he opens the first box." I checked the time on my cell phone. "But you don't have to stick around. I can watch the gift shop since I'm staying late anyway."

Lindsay snapped upright from her elbow-propped slouch over a glass jewelry case and flipped her long blonde hair over her shoulder. "Really? Then I could get my bangs trimmed before the gals at the Golden Shears close." She rustled in a cupboard for her purse. "Are you coming to the game tomorrow night?"

"Depends on what's in the shipment."

"We're going to state again, for sure. It'll be a great game—you won't want to miss it." Lindsay blew an air kiss and dashed out.

Late-summer sunlight poured through the greenish-tinted glass double doors, illuminating dust motes swirling in Lindsay's wake. Technically it was autumn, but some days were still hitting the eighties in the middle of the Columbia River Gorge.

Hot days and cool nights. Football weather—in a town where high school football is the source of more speculation and gossipy predictions than extramarital affairs or petty crime.

Looking for cleaning supplies, I opened a deep drawer under the cash register. Lindsay had stashed the leftover refrigerator magnets in there, next to the feather duster. Well, that was smart, actually.

The magnet display rack, ordered by some enterprising—but long-gone—staff member, had taken up a lot of space. With only three Ermas, one Gayle, one Gail, and two Deloreses left, it had been an eyesore—a petered-out tourist trinket trap. Lindsay has a natural knack for merchandising. The gift shop seems less cluttered under her management.

I flitted the feather duster over cramped shelves of history, geology, and native flora and fauna books, Umatilla and Chinook jewelry stands, stacks of puzzles, the hanging display of novelty kites, and greeting card and postcard carousel racks. Dust billowed, and I sneezed into the crook of my arm.

It's not that we don't clean—we do, all the time. But the Imogene is old, and she has cracks—having been built long before anything was airtight and energy efficient. And with the way the wind blows in the gorge, silt spills in one side while we're sweeping it out the other.

No visitors came—not surprising for a late-September Thursday afternoon. Not really surprising for the Imogene Museum, either. Our odd assortment of folk art, fine art, textiles, and random collections of whatever catches Rupert Hagg's eye doesn't draw large crowds, even on the best day.

It's the kind of museum that flea market aficionados love, if they can find the tiny dot of Platts Landing, Washington, on the map—because Rupert, the director, purchased most of the Imogene's treasures from flea markets around the world. Or he scrounged through estate sales, antique gallery liquidation sales, and the like. Every once in a while he's been able to wheedle entire collections from people in dire straits or from those who discovered their grandchildren weren't interested in inheriting ceramic napkin rings or elephant carvings or miniature steam engines or whatnot.

I stepped to the front doors to lock them at six p.m.

Ford Huckle stood suddenly from beyond the shrubs flanking the entrance sidewalk. I tried to stifle my surprised screech, but he heard enough through the thick glass to look my way. I waved.

He waved back, enormous scissorlike pruning shears still in his hand. His sparse salt-and-pepper hair stuck out in ruffled tufts, like the feathers of those fancy bantam roosters. He grinned, revealing several gaps between his teeth, wiped his free hand on the front of his dirty olive drab coveralls, and bent to resume snipping.

Ford is genial and well intentioned, but he becomes a little lost outside of his routine responsibilities. He's a fixture at the museum, with a long-standing connection only Rupert fully understands, and lives on the grounds in an old pump house that was converted into a cabin.

I pushed the doors open. "Hey, Ford."

Ford stood again. "Missus Morehouse."

I had tried to explain to Ford that I'm not married, but the concept hadn't sunk in. All women are "Missus" to him. At least he's consistent.

"The shrubs look nice."

"They'll stop growin' soon. It's gettin' cold nights," Ford answered.

"You going to the football game tomorrow?"

"You bet." Ford grinned again. "Goin' t' see Missus Lindsay's young man wallop those Senators."

I laughed.

"They're gettin' cocky, those Senators. Need a good wallopin'." Ford nodded.

"Greg's coming tonight to help me unpack the new shipment. Will you keep an eye out for him? Tell him I'm in the basement?"

"Greg's comin'? Well, how-dee-do. It's not Friday."

"Nope. It's a special treat."

"All right. I gotta git back to work." Ford presented his saggy, pocketed posterior and recommenced clipping.

I locked the front doors and skipped down the creaky stairs to the museum's basement. Low-ceilinged and cavernous, it holds decades' worth of broken display cases, unidentified artifacts, orphan furniture, and, weirdly, a matching avocado washer-and-dryer set. I needed to post them on Craigslist and pass them on to someone who would actually use them, if they still worked.

But the main attraction was the pile of twenty-three boxes strapped with yellow DHL tape. Rupert had sent them from Munich three weeks ago, and they'd been delayed in customs for almost another week. I'd had half a mind to march to Seattle and kick those customs officials in the seat myself, but instead I'd nearly worn out my computer tracking the shipment multiple times per day.

Rupert goes on several buying trips every year, delighting in keeping the contents of his new collections secret until they arrive. I would like the chance to preorder display cases in the right sizes, but this eccentricity of Rupert's does make unpacking like Christmas—not the reserved, grown-up version of Christmas where everyone puts their name and wish list in a basket and you know you'll be receiving what you asked for, but rather like that glorious, if hazy, dream of Christmas where you go downstairs in your footie pajamas, rubbing sleep out of your eyes, and there's the sparkling pocketknife or toy rocket launcher or volcano kit you've been pestering your parents about for months.

Except, with Rupert, the premier item might be a deep-sea diving helmet or a mimeograph machine or an intricate Celtic knot twined from a dead person's hair.

Greg, who's studying anthropology and loves all things dusty and unusual, has been infected by the anticipation and had begged to be present at the grand opening. So I forced myself to do the one thing I am worst at doing—waiting.

I propped open the basement door to let in fresh air. Then I dragged the boxes into two parallel rows and wheeled padded transit carts into position—ready to cradle the new collection.

Greg and I had been plodding through the stored collections, documenting them and moving them into public view so the museum's massive rooms looked less bare. The work was sometimes tedious and always too slow for my taste, but I suppose the Imogene, as a gatekeeper of history, is patient about improvements.

The ballroom, with its parquet oak floor, echoes so loudly that I'm desperate for a textile display to absorb some of the sound. I had given Rupert instructions to this effect when he left for Europe, but he operates on whim, not necessity, and so could not be counted on to follow through. Besides, the boxes were all squarish. I didn't hold out hope they contained rolled tapestries or quilts.

"Helloo?" Greg's voice sounded outside.

"Down here," I shouted.

The stimulating odor of pepperoni wafted in with Greg. "It's not hot anymore, but I picked up a pizza in The Dalles." He dropped his backpack and set the pizza box on a transit cart.

"You're the best." I flipped the lid open and dug in.

"That I am," Greg said around a mouthful, "considering I drove all the way here without sneaking a slice. So?" He gestured toward the boxes. "Any idea what's in them?"

"The honor's all yours." I handed him a box knife.

Greg grinned and gingerly sliced through the tape on the closest box. He pulled out wads of packing paper, then a bubble-wrapped object. He peeled back layers of protective plastic to reveal a double-handled pot. It was covered in a transferware design of gaudy rose bouquets and had a gilt rim.

I gasped.

"What?" Greg asked. "It's pretty, right?"

"It's a chamber pot. Oh, no . . . no . . . no." I pawed through the box and came up with two more bubble-wrapped items of similar size. "Oh, no."

Oh, yes. Chamber pots and bedpans. Seventy-two of them.

Greg lost it at number eighteen. He chuckled uncontrollably as we lined up chamber pot after chamber pot on the transit carts. "Should we group them by style?" he asked. "Florals versus strictly utilitarian? Landscapes and country scenes? How about the ones with urinal spouts? Oh, look—a miniature pot." He held up a child-size basic version in white-spotted cobalt-blue enamel.

I plopped on the floor amid piles of packing material. "Well, that's a thought. We could present this as a 'what life was like before indoor plumbing' exhibit, suitable for all ages. Kids might really get a kick out of it. The first potty chairs were for grown-ups, too."

"You should get one of those modern plastic numbers, just to show how much things have, or rather have not, changed over the years."

I tossed a wad of Bubble Wrap at him, and missed. "They'll fit in standard dishware display cases. Although I think we should leave a few out for an interactive display. There are a couple here that aren't too valuable—for a hands-on experience."

"You mean a butt-on experience. They can't be comfortable." Greg squatted above an enamelware model registered at the United States Patent and Trademark Office, according to a label crackled and peeling with age. He perched precariously, his lanky frame tripled up, knees to chin, arms outstretched for balance.

"You're behaving like the teenage brother I missed the pleasure of having." I laughed. "You want to give the tour? Try explaining how an American chamber pot ended up in Germany. Did a family love it so much they had to take it with them on vacation? Maybe it belonged to a diplomat, and he wasn't sure what kind of facilities would be available in his new country of residence."

Greg shoved his glasses up on his nose and staggered to his feet. "Nope. That's your department. Dibs on the last piece of pizza." He kicked at some stray packing paper. "Then let's get this junk out of here."

We dragged the flattened cardboard boxes through the cricket-chorused night—the little creatures' last hurrah before they hibernated or whatever it is they do during the winter. The recycling dumpster sat under a buzzing halogen floodlight. Bugs swarmed in the light shaft, eddying upward to slam against the glass lamp.

"Thanks so much for helping," I said. "I feel bad that you're driving up from Corvallis every weekend. You must not have a social life."

"Nah. It doesn't matter." Greg turned, beads of sweat glistening on his scalp through his close-cropped brown hair. "Angie's in Turkey this quarter, on a dig."

I hadn't met Greg's new girlfriend, and I still didn't like her. Something to do with the way Greg puppy-dogged about Angie, like he was intimidated by her yet panted faithfully at her heels all the same. I wrinkled my nose. "Is Dr. Elroy giving you independent credit for this term as well as summer term? I'd be happy to fill out assessments for you—whatever you need."

"Yeah, I expect he'll e-mail you in a few weeks. He's not big on paperwork."

"My kind of guy." I followed Greg down the ramp.

"Yeah, you might like Dr. Elroy. I've had him for a couple classes, but this internship is way better than sitting through lectures."

"I *might* like him?"

"I have a feeling he's a lot more interesting outside the classroom than he is in it. Angie TA'd for him last year, and they really hit it off. We weren't dating then, but she told me about a couple cool research projects she got to do for him. They were on a first-name basis. I still get the impression he wouldn't like me calling him Clyde." Greg grinned. "But I'm sure he'd love to talk shop with a professional peer. Besides, you're a borderline museum hermit, you know. All you do is work. Maybe you need an intervention."

"What, and give up communing with chamber pots? Really, Greg."

He chuckled and surveyed the transit carts with his hands on his bony hips. "So, plan of action?"

"I think oldest to newest. Let's document each one, circa date and maker, location of use if possible, any interesting history about the companies who made them."

"Celebrity endorsements?"

"If you can find a photo of someone important sitting on a pot just like one of these, I'll give you a raise."

"Considering that I work for free, I'll take cookies or your carrot cake with the really thick frosting."

"Deal. We've done enough for tonight, though."

I trudged upstairs to my office on the third floor. Greg followed with the stack of packing slips.

My office had once been planned as a child's nursery. Rupert's great-great-uncle built the mansion as an idyllic vacation home in anticipation of a large extended family that never materialized. Apart from the occasional high-society party, it sat in hollow emptiness for many years until the trust fund found another purpose for it.

The room is light and airy during the day, with a huge picture window providing a breathtaking view of the Columbia River Gorge. The walls are lined with packed bookcases (the trust fund splurges on my book allowance), the rows of books two deep on many shelves.

A solitary green light blinked through the black window, a channel marker for boat traffic on the river below. I flipped on the desk lamp. Greg slid the packing slips under my Murano glass paperweight and stepped to the shelves.

"Do you have anything on the geological history of the Columbia Gorge and Native American culture in the area?"

"Yeah." I pointed to the sections. "I wish we had more exhibits of local historical significance. It's a shame that we have chamber pots from Germany but no Chinook, Wishram, or Klickitat artifacts from before the Lewis and Clark expedition."

"You know, Angie would be able to sniff some out. She's amazing. I should bring her up here when she gets back." Greg's face looked a little pinched—was he worried?

I tried to keep a polite nuance to my grunt.

He slid books off a shelf. "Okay if I borrow these?"

"Sure, just write down the titles and pin the note to the corkboard on the back of the door," I replied. "My sophisticated checkout system."

Greg perused for another half hour while I e-mailed Rupert to let him know the shipment had arrived at last and intact. I included a reminder nudge about a textile exhibit and suggested tapestries since he was, or had been recently, in Germany. Rupert's itinerary is always as impulsive as his purchases.

And I couldn't resist looking up a few of the chamber pots to scan for histories and dates—just something to get us started in the morning.

We clumped down to the main floor and crossed the ballroom exhibit hall in the gloom. The after-hours lighting system kept us from banging our shins on things, but it made the display cases look like encircling giants waiting for the signal to pounce. I could walk through the museum blindfolded, so they didn't bother me. The giants were old friends.

Greg shuffled a little, as though distracted.

Our footsteps bounced back from all directions. The room felt smaller when you couldn't see the walls.

"You seem tired," I said, missing his usual banter.

"It's a long drive. Guess I'm ready to crash."

"So are you going to the game tomorrow?"

"Uh, I'd like to. Are you?"

"I think so. Now that I've seen what's in the shipment, I think it's manageable. The annual school tours start next week, and I'd love to have the display ready for them. I'll warn the principal so she can head off any parental complaints about the, uh—basic—nature of the exhibit."

"Aw, they're kids. They'll be fascinated."

Greg looks like a vertically stretched version of the one owlish, bookish kid in every fourth-grade class who can seriously recite Thomas Crapper's contributions to sanitation.

I set the alarm and bolted the doors behind us.

Greg inhaled deeply as we walked to the parking lot. "Early?"

"I'll be here at seven. Come when you've had enough sleep."

Greg lodges with Betty Jenkins on the weekends. The Jenkins homestead is humble but sturdy enough to withstand the vibrations from the two-, three-, and four-engine freight trains that thunder by at all hours of the night and day.

The Columbia River Gorge is a commerce thoroughfare—traversed by barge, rail, and Jake-braking semitrucks on highways along both banks. Sounds carry miles over the water. The residents are accustomed to the noise, forget to notice after a while. But Greg has to work at getting acclimated every weekend.

I climbed into my pickup and listened with satisfaction as the engine came to life with a throaty growl. Greg accordioned into his

Toyota Prius. When his headlights came on, I pulled out of my spot and drove along the access road to State Route 14. The museum property borders the county park, and they share the large parking lot.

I turned left onto the highway and watched in my rearview mirror until Greg turned right, toward town. I couldn't shake the feeling that something was bothering him.

CHAPTER 2

When I pulled into spot C-17 at the Riverview RV Ranch, a leggy, long-eared hound eased her lean body through the open door of her kennel, tail wagging in a lazy clockwise circle.

"Hey, Tuppence, old girl, sorry I'm late." I scratched the dog's white-and-black-speckled back while she took inventory of my pant legs and shoes.

Inspection complete, I unlocked the door to my fifth-wheel trailer and let Tuppence climb the two steps ahead of me. The hound is a recent addition to the home landscape. She'd been Wirt Maple's dog. But last spring, when, for the first time in thirty years, Wirt failed to show up at the Junction General Store on a Saturday to do his weekly shopping, Gloria Munoz, owner of the Junction, called Sheriff Marge Stettler. And Sheriff Marge drove forty-eight miles into the hills to find the leathery old farmer dead in his rocking chair, with Tuppence, nose on paws beside him, starting to starve.

Sheriff Marge brought the dog back and dropped her off at my place, saying she knew of "two girls who could use each other's company." And that was that. I named the hound after one of Agatha

Christie's curious sleuths—I happened to be reading *By the Pricking of My Thumbs* that night.

The RV's a hand-me-down from a dead guy, too, sort of. When I took the curator position at the museum and started looking for a place to live, I discovered that rental housing was nonexistent in Platts Landing. A snarky colleague—actually the man who was stepping in to fill the coveted director-of-marketing position I'd just quit—joked that living in the boonies meant you had to take your home with you, like a turtle. And he was right.

I found a deal on a six-year-old, but never-used, luxury fifth-wheel trailer from the widow of the man who'd bought it for his retirement and then promptly died of a massive heart attack. It had been parked in the widow's driveway until she could bear to part with it, the memories of their dreams and plans for travel too strong to fade quickly.

The fully restored burgundy 1972 Chevy Cheyenne to tow the trailer came the next day, from a macho young man oh-so-sorry to see the baby that was older than he was drive away. But he was desperate for cash, and I needed the horsepower.

I had a fifth-wheel hitch installed in the pickup's bed, packed the few belongings I hadn't given away, turned the house keys over to the Realtor, and bid good riddance to my city life.

I hadn't regretted it for a moment.

And I wouldn't let myself do that. No matter what.

"You want some of the stinky canned stuff of questionable origin?"

Tuppence answered with a few tail thumps.

"I thought so. You're so predictable." I plunked Tuppence's metal food bowl on the hardwood floor.

I arched my back and stretched from side to side while a cheese sandwich sizzled on the griddle. Chamber pots aren't heavy, but all the stooping and rummaging through boxes had taken their toll on my neglected muscles. Tuppence and Greg were right—I needed to get out more. Maybe when the new exhibit was finished.

I sank into one of the recliners and poked a button to turn on the gas fireplace. The big picture window above the fireplace showed a black hole tonight, but the inky Columbia River slid by a few feet away.

Tuppence swung her long body over, front and back halves working independently, and sat with her nose resting on my knee. She watched every bite, eyebrows raised to track my hand from plate to mouth.

"Yes, I do feel guilty, but I'm not sharing. I only had two slices of pizza, and that was hours ago." I wiped my fingers on my jeans, and Tuppence consoled herself with sniffing the greasy streak for crumbs.

My body had stiffened in a semi-bent position. I groaned, kicked the footrest down, and pushed out of the warm depths of the chair.

I tidied a few things while Tuppence made her nightly rounds. When she snuffled at the door, I let her back in and pulled her dog bed from under the sofa. She sniffed all over to make sure it was the same as last night, then flopped down, ears splayed, eyes closed. I would let her sleep in the bedroom except she snores. Sometimes she dream-sniffs and -snorts like she's flushing out a rabbit or fox—or an elephant, if volume is any indicator.

I patted the dog's side, then padded upstairs to the bedroom and slid the pocket door closed. Living in a fifth-wheel is like living in a split-level—up half a flight of stairs to the high portion that extends over the towing pickup's bed.

The alarm buzzed before daylight, but I rolled out of bed without hitting the snooze button, my brain already leaping ahead to what the day held in store. I showered fast in the narrow cubbyhole of a shower stall and welcomed the coffee aroma drifting in from the kitchen.

I finger-combed my wet brown curls in a fruitless effort to tame them. Barbara at the Golden Shears had called it a no-fuss pixie cut. I only cared that it was wash-and-wear.

I leaned into the mirror for a closer look at the freckles that had popped out over the summer. But what was the point in bothering about them, since nothing changed anyway? After swiping on mascara and blush to give my pale face some color, I dressed in layers for a day that would go from cold to hot to cold and then to downright freezing on the metal bleachers at the football game.

When I slid open the bedroom door, Tuppence raised her head, realized nothing exciting was happening, and let her head drop back on the pillow. I poured a mug of coffee with whole milk and brown sugar and ate breakfast in front of the laptop. Remembering the chamber pot label claiming a US patent, I did a quick patent search. Expired—of course.

Tuppence staggered over and sat with her chin on my thigh. I stroked her head, making a mental checklist for the day.

I don't have the educational background to be a museum curator—my MBA is a long way from a degree in anthropology, history, or archeology—but curating is in my blood. I have to work harder at research than someone who's been trained in the profession, but I love everything about my job—fact-finding, categorizing, creating order and meaning from mismatched objects, solving puzzles, and sharing discoveries. Seeing visitors' reactions when they learn what life was like for people similar to them but who lived generations ago gives me a rush of satisfaction. If Rupert weren't paying me, I'd still find a way to volunteer.

I glanced at the clock and jumped from my seat, sending Tuppence sprawling. "Sorry, old girl."

I scrambled to clean up the breakfast mess and dashed outside to fill Tuppence's bowls with kibble and clean water.

"Eat up before the squirrels get it."

Tuppence snorted.

I drove out of the campground as quietly as possible. There were no signs of life yet outside the cluster of tents staked in the Russian olive grove or around the huge motor coach from Tennessee. Tourist traffic was dwindling and soon I'd be the only resident of Riverview Ranch except Herb and Harriet Tinsley, the elderly twins who live in the original farmhouse and maintain the campground that was their grandparents' homestead.

I brought the Chevy up to speed on the highway and scanned the misty pink horizon where it filtered into gold, pale blue, and then deep cobalt with tinges of violet. I leaned forward to peer up through the bug-splattered windshield and couldn't keep from smiling. Sunrises in the city are dismal affairs compared to this.

Just as I turned onto the tree-lined city park road, bronze rays flashed over the distant hills and chased all the other colors away. Brilliant light strobed between tree trunks as I wound closer to the river's edge and parked.

Mica in the Imogene Museum's greenish-gray stone walls sparkled in the sun. The mansion staggers up and up, three stories aboveground like blocks a toddler has arranged in a pile—a surprisingly modern form for its having been built in 1902. Cubism in architecture a few years before cubism showed up in paintings by Picasso and Braque—probably unrelated, but I like to dream that the museum's anonymous architect was a friend of Picasso's.

I arranged a workstation in the basement with a couple of folding chairs and my laptop on a card table. I pulled over a spotlight on a rolling stand and used a digital camera to click documentation photos of all seventy-two chamber pots. Greg arrived and set about assigning an identification number to each piece.

I called Mac MacDougal as soon as I thought it was polite, considering he's the owner of the only tavern in town and likely awake until the wee hours. Mac's first love is his woodworking shop behind the tavern. He lives in the loft of the big pole building and spends his free time puttering around with power tools.

"Yeah?" Mac croaked into the phone.

"Sorry, Mac. Did I wake you?"

"Nope. Just hadn't used my voice yet today. Got a job for me? I heard you got a shipment."

"Yup. Five standard display cases with three glass shelves each, full lighting."

"I've worked ahead, so I already have three standards on hand. Just waiting for the glass shelves. I can finish the others by Tuesday, probably."

"Mac, you're a wonder. I owe you."

"You could come have a pint with me."

"Oh, uh, well, I'll see you Sunday at the potluck." I hung up.

Shoot—not Mac, too. As a single woman in Sockeye County, I'm overwhelmingly outnumbered by single men. The ratio in the thirty-to-sixty age group is probably five to one. I'm surrounded by lonely farmers, wind-farm technicians, mechanics, truckers, railroad workers, and bartenders. Although *surrounded* is a loose term, given the sparse population.

I went back to shuffling chamber pots into chronological order.

I took Greg to lunch at the marina's Burger Basket & Bait Shop. While we waited, Greg stared out the window at the few fishermen who dozed in lawn chairs on the floating walkway. He had dark circles under his eyes, and his face was slack. I know graduate school can be torturous, and most students have a dazed appearance that increases the closer they get to giving their defense. But Greg had appeared to be handling the pressure with equanimity—until now.

When our food arrived, I dunked a couple of fries into tartar sauce and stuffed them in my mouth. Greg, who normally ate like he was packing Mary Poppins's carpetbag, dismembered his parsley sprig garnish.

"You've been quiet today. Rough night?" I asked.

Greg didn't respond, so I kicked him under the table.

His head popped up. "Huh?"

"What's wrong? Trains keep you awake?"

"Nah. Angie e-mailed."

"And?"

"Ever since she got to Turkey, she's been raving about this guy, Lorenzo—a professor of something or other from Florence who's on the same dig. She thinks he's a genius." Greg ran his thumb through the condensation on his water glass. "With my luck, he probably has those dark Italian good looks, wears pointy shoes, and drives a Ferrari."

"I think he's short, balding, flat-footed, has an enormous hook nose, and drives his mother's Fiat. His belly hangs below his belt, and he's bowlegged. He has halitosis and obvious earwax." I cocked my head. "Shall I keep going?"

Greg snorted. "No. But thank you."

"Anytime."

As we sauntered back to the museum, I caught a glimpse of the Port of Platts Landing's grain elevators through the trees. Pete Sills's tug had a barge bumped against the pilings. He usually managed to be in town for the home football games. I considered hunkering in my trailer that night instead.

CHAPTER 3

I spent the afternoon weaving facts and anecdotes into descriptions for the chamber pots. A detailed history of the pre–indoor plumbing days emerged, showing how manufacturers tried to spruce up the basic equipment with designs that were more and more elaborate.

Greg took on the task of entering the pots into the database and matching the identification records with the photos. I looked up several times to find him staring into space, mouth drawn into a frown.

Angie's infatuation with another man must have been gnawing at him. Or was there something else? I considered asking but hated to be openly nosy. He'd talk when he was ready, I hoped.

I stretched my arms toward the ceiling, then rubbed the back of my neck.

"Ready to call it quits?" Greg asked.

"Yeah. I love how this exhibit proves anything can be interesting if you learn enough about it."

"That's how it is for me and football. Never played, didn't understand the rules, but the enthusiasm in this town is contagious. Now I know a touchdown is seven points."

"Six," I said. "Then one more point if they kick the ball through the goalposts afterward. Or two more points if—"

"Oh." Greg shrugged. "Well, I'm getting there."

"If you need a tutor, sit by Lindsay. She's a football encyclopedia."

I packed my laptop but left everything else in place for the next day's marathon session.

"See you at the game," Greg said, making a break for the door.

"Mmm." I kept my mumble noncommittal.

I locked up and trudged to my truck. The game might be just the thing to cheer Greg up, help him forget his girl trouble for a few hours.

But at the age of thirty-three, I don't consider myself eligible to have man trouble. How could I have man trouble when the man is oblivious anyway? Sure, I thwart the halfhearted requests for dates from lethargic, lonely males—that's easy. But then there's Pete. He isn't lethargic, doesn't seem to be lonely, and barely acknowledges my existence. All terribly irritating.

"Oh, grow up," I muttered as I turned the key in the pickup's ignition.

After feeding Tuppence and grilling another cheese sandwich, I pulled on my rattiest old sweats and wool socks.

"Don't you think avoidance of Pete Sills is the best course of action?" I asked the dog.

Tuppence swung her tail in a low arc.

"Yeah, I figured you'd side with him. But you're not rendered weak-kneed by crinkle-cornered blue eyes and chronic three-day stubble, are you?"

Tuppence licked her chops.

"Oh. So maybe you are."

I sat on the floor in front of the fireplace with Tuppence's head on my knee and the laptop open beside me. Next up was an enameled graniteware chamber pot, bucket-style, with lid. Lids on chamber pots really were innovative at the time. I slid into curator mode and typed:

> What would you do with a chamber pot in the morning? If you were wealthy, you probably had a maid who would empty it, clean it, and slip it back under your bed. If you weren't rich, you had to do the chore yourself. At first people took the easy way and flung the contents of the chamber pot out the window. That was generally not appreciated by other folks in town if there was a walkway under your window. Common courtesy demanded chamber pots be emptied in the privy or outhouse. Lids were a fairly late addition to chamber pot technology and ensured the contents remained secure on the journey to the privy.

Sharp rapping rattled the door. I jumped, and Tuppence let out a muffled "Mmmrf," as if embarrassed she'd been caught napping. I pushed her off my lap and creaked my sore joints to standing.

A voice outside called, "Hellooo?" Pete Sills's voice.

My heart went into spin cycle, and I looked down at the torn knees of my sweat pants. Classy, suave, sophisticated—not. I took a deep breath. Why worry about what Pete Sills thought?

I flung open the door.

Pete, in his rough red-and-black buffalo plaid jacket, Carhartt pants, and steel-toed work boots, looked straight into my eyes. "You going to the game? I could use a lift."

I sighed. Since my reason for avoiding the game was standing on the doorstep, there was no need to maintain the charade. "Yeah. I need to change first."

Pete took a step up, meaning to come in. "I'll wait."

"No," I snapped. "Outside. You'll wait outside."

Tuppence wriggled through the doorway to greet Pete. Of course, *she* loved him. She had a thing for men, the dirtier the better. Pete's pants were stained with machine grease.

Pete arched his brows, an amused smile flickering across his face. He shrugged and stepped back to the welcome mat and stuffed his hands in his pockets. I slammed the door and dove for the bedroom.

I yanked off my comfortable lounge-around clothes, pulled on the jeans and sweater worn earlier, and stuffed my feet into my warmest hiking boots. A quick look at my face and hair in the mirror—but there was nothing I could salvage in short order.

I cringed, remembering how thin RV walls are. Pete probably knew exactly what all the shuffling and lurching inside was accomplishing. I muttered silently about his persistent inopportuneness while I grabbed a puffy down jacket, a hat, and a rawhide treat for Tuppence.

Pete was leaning against the passenger-side door of my truck. He'd already loaded his bicycle in the bed, with one handlebar hooked over the tailgate. He kept the bike on his tugboat and used it for trips into nearby towns when he stopped to load and unload barges. I realized the high school football field was too far away to pedal to in the dark.

He smiled. He had very white teeth against his dark stubble. Probably wore braces as a kid. Maybe I should go easier on him. Maybe.

I opened the driver's door and climbed in. Pete slid onto the bench seat from the other side, smelling faintly of licorice and dusty wheat. His large frame took up more than his half of the seat. And then I discovered I didn't have the keys.

I tumbled out of the truck, found I hadn't locked the trailer door, either, grabbed the keys from the hook inside, and locked the trailer, a residual big-city habit. Probably not necessary out here, but it made me feel better—when I remembered to do it. Although it would have been deathly mortifying tonight if I'd remembered to lock the trailer with my truck keys still inside. The image of Pete pedaling to Junction General with me balanced on the handlebars so we could borrow jimmying tools made my stomach lurch.

I scooted back into the truck. Pete didn't say a word, which irritated me even more. Why did the man make me so flustered? It was just so stupid. I clamped my gloved hands around the steering wheel and resolved to be more mature.

We drove to the stadium in silence. I thought about starting a conversation, but everything seemed ridiculous after my brainless escapade. It wouldn't be helpful to reveal more scatteredness by opening my mouth. Good thing my truck is kind of noisy.

Pete paid for my ticket before I could argue and led me toward the packed bleachers.

"Meredith! Over here."

Greg's arms windmilled about halfway up at midfield. I hoped he'd saved only one seat. But when the friendly crowd saw two were trying to squeeze in, they moved over and adjusted their seat cushions to make room. Pete pressed in, fitting on the end of the bench—shoulder, hip, and thigh tight against me. My stomach flip-flopped.

Lindsay reached across Greg and patted my knee. "I'm so glad you came."

I was only able to nod back over the roar of the crowd as the home team took the field.

The Platts Landing Polecats gave the Sheldon Senators the walloping Ford claimed they needed. Lindsay hollered like the cheerleader she used to be, getting our entire section into the groove. Lindsay's boyfriend, the quarterback, ran in for the team's fifth touchdown with just seconds remaining in the half, and the team went to the locker room, ahead 35–3.

Pete stumped down the metal stairs into the celebrating throng. I shivered in the sudden chilliness caused by his absence. I'd forgotten he was there in my enthusiasm for the game and hadn't realized he'd been blocking the wind. I hunched into my coat and listened to Lindsay explain the offside penalty to Greg.

"Brilliant. You should do sports broadcasting. Your explanations are easy to understand," Greg said.

I leaned in. "Yep. I told him he should sit by you so he could learn the game."

Lindsay beamed, then flushed. "When you grow up with a bunch of brothers and a dad who are crazy about football, you can't help it. It's the only thing I know much about."

"Aw, come on." Greg wrapped his arm around her shoulders. "I bet you know lots of stuff. You just haven't had the chance to show it yet."

This time Lindsay's blush went deep into her hair. I leaned back and smiled. Good-bye, Angie—maybe.

Pete reclaimed his spot and handed me a loaded hot dog and a can of Barq's root beer. "You don't like cola, right?"

"Right. Thanks." How did he remember that? Was he paying attention, or was it a fluke?

Anyway, the hot dog was great. Ambience is vital for hot dogs. They taste good only when charred over a campfire or at football games when your team is ahead. Smothered in sauerkraut, onions, and mustard, this one hit the spot.

I licked my lips and grinned at the fact that I certainly wouldn't have kissable breath tonight. Take that, Pete Sills. Not that he'd ever tried. Maybe he didn't like my freckles. Or how I always acted so ditzy around him. Well, if those were his problems, he was too shallow to waste time thinking about.

Yeah, right.

The Senators staged a short-lived rally late in the third, causing a fumble near the goal line and intercepting a line-drive pass, but the Polecats pulled off a 42–17 win. The crowd slapped one another on the back, yawned, stretched, and cascaded down the bleachers.

A man in a blazer, khakis, and loafers stood on the sideline, talking to Lindsay's boyfriend. He was definitely not a local—not in that getup. He had to be a college scout. I felt a twinge of pity for Lindsay. The girl was about to be left behind by a boyfriend already two years her junior. She needed a stick of ambition dynamite lit under her. Maybe Greg could do that. Maybe he already had.

Pete and I moved with the flow toward the parking lot. My behind was numb from the cold, hard bleacher seat and tingly from fresh blood flow. No hip-sashaying motion here. More like a chicken waddle.

I wrinkled my nose at a whiff of marijuana wafting from the group in front of us—a mix of high-schoolers and parents. Didn't people have sense enough not to smoke pot at such a public event and in front of kids? Or maybe it was the kids. Then where were their parents?

I sighed—I was sinking into indignant old-woman mode.

The slapping sound of big, flat feet pounding the pavement rushed up behind me. I sidestepped quickly.

"Missus Morehouse," Ford panted.

"Hi, Ford."

"Can I get a ride with you? Mac brought me, but he has to stay for a while. I don't want to wait."

"Sure. Your prediction about the game came true."

Ford grinned and tapped his temple. "I know things."

Pete chuckled. "Do you predict final scores, too? 'Cause I know a guy who could set us up if you have that kind of information."

"Pete. Don't you dare."

Pete shrugged and grinned.

"I don't gamble," Ford said. "That'll get you in trouble. And if you do that, they take things away, like your house and your car and your family. Course, I don't have those things, but jes' the same, it's wicked, and I don't do it."

"Hear, hear," I muttered, and wondered how Ford had gained this knowledge.

"Point taken," Pete said, quickly serious.

"That's right." Ford nodded.

We crammed into the pickup, with Ford in the middle. I turned the heater on full blast, and gradually became aware that Ford's hygiene lacked a little something. Hints of irate raccoon plus the permeating odor of moldy potatoes made my eyes water.

I really shouldn't know what irate raccoon smells like, but thanks to Tuppence, I do.

After a few miles, I decided the tangy fragrance might not emanate from Ford personally, but rather his clothes. Perhaps they just needed a good scrubbing. The image of the unused avocado washer and dryer in the museum basement popped into my head. I'd talk to Rupert when he returned, see if they could be installed in Ford's cabin. But didn't he already have laundry facilities?

I turned onto the straight, wide road leading to the port. Ford's cabin was closer to the port than to the museum parking lot. It didn't have an access road, so Ford would have to walk no matter where I dropped him off. I pulled up next to the dock where Pete's tug was anchored.

We all climbed out. Ford took off cross-country at a fast clip, waving his hand once. Pete hoisted his bike out of the truck bed.

"Do you think he's okay, living by himself in that shack?" he asked.

"I don't know."

Pete grunted. "I forgot. We're not the best people to judge. You live by yourself in an RV. I live alone on a tugboat. We're probably all a little crazy." He wheeled the bike down the dock.

I climbed back into the truck and drove home with the windows down. I resented Pete's observation. I couldn't possibly be crazy, because I don't live alone. I live with Tuppence.

CHAPTER 4

Still steamed from Pete's comment, I knew I wouldn't be falling asleep anytime soon. So I decided to focus my restless energy on carrot cake. The day had been productive. If Saturday went just as well, Greg and I could take Sunday off.

Tuppence hid under the dining table while I whacked pecans into tiny pieces with a butcher knife.

"What's wrong with you?"

She thumped her tail but did not come out. I gave the chopping board another bang, making nuts bounce all over the counter.

"Oh." I put the knife down and peered under the table. "It's not me, is it? Am I making you nervous?"

Tuppence whined and stuck her cold nose in my face.

"I see. Sorry, old girl. You know I get worked up about Pete."

I grated carrots, drained a can of crushed pineapple, and measured out raisins and the other ingredients. After placing the cake in the oven, I sat on the floor and pulled Tuppence onto my lap. The big dog worked her bony knees and hips into a comfortable position and let me stroke her long, silky ears.

I bent my head down to look in Tuppence's sad eyes. "I'm not crazy, am I?"

Not normally a licking dog, she swiped my chin with her tongue.

"Thank you," I whispered. I slumped back against the refrigerator and closed my eyes.

The timer jolted me awake. The RV smelled of cinnamon and a fruity sweetness. My legs had fallen asleep under the hound's weight. I slowly rose and pushed my fists into my lower back muscles.

"I have to improve my posture," I groaned. "I cannot be getting old."

I set the pans on a rack to cool. After snitching a corner of cake, I tumbled into bed.

The alarm came too soon, but the lingering spicy scent reminded me of the waiting frosting job. I rolled out of bed and rushed through my morning routine.

I whipped cream cheese with powdered sugar and an overdose of vanilla. A dollop of frosting in my coffee was my splurge for the day. I hummed "Louie Louie"—still stuck in my head from last night. It was the only song the high school marching band had fully mastered, and they played it with gusto.

Greg would be driving back to school in Corvallis the next day, so I cut the cake into quarters and packaged each section in its own airtight plastic container. Then I collected my things and made the short commute to the museum.

When Greg arrived we resurrected a bed frame and mattress from the basement, loaded them into the freight elevator, and dragged them into a bedroom on the second floor—the new chamber pot exhibit room. Then Greg ran heavy-duty extension cords for the display cases Mac was building.

I found an ancient coverlet and a couple of down pillows in the stash of family linens still housed in the original servants' quarters. I made the bed and slid the enamelware specimen just under the edge so it was still visible.

"Perfecto," Greg said.

I stood back to survey the effect. "Yeah. I thought it would be a nice touch."

"History isn't stuffy and boring when it's interactive." Greg nodded. "This makes me glad I switched majors."

"I didn't know that. From what?"

"You'll laugh."

"No, I won't."

"Well, you'll be amused, anyway. Music—piano performance. I have the hands for it"—he wiggled his long fingers—"but not enough talent."

"That explains your comprehensive knowledge of early jazz."

Greg grinned. "Music is an important part of culture, so I guess it wasn't such a big leap to cultural anthropology."

"I've seen how excited you get about research—I think you've found a home."

"And you need an oak Victorian throne-style chair with a hole in the seat for holding a chamber pot to round out this collection."

"So—find us a good one on eBay." I shook my head, grinning. "And remind me never to break into song in your presence. I might offend your musical sensibilities."

After lunch we finished the individual descriptions for each chamber pot and printed them on heavy card stock. Greg laminated the ones that would be hung on the wall or tented to stand next to the chamber pots that were out for public handling. I sorted the rest of the cards into order.

"That's it. Can't do anything else until Mac delivers the cases."

Greg set the stack of laminated cards on my desk. "I'm bummed I'm going to miss the final setup."

"I'll send pictures to your phone. Oh, and these are for you." I pulled the cake containers out of the mini fridge under my desk. "Thanks so much. I know the school kids are going to love this exhibit. I couldn't have had it ready in time without you."

Greg cracked a lid open. "Carrot? Meredith, you're the best."

"Really? I've been thinking I might be crazy."

Greg scowled. "Something I should know about?"

"Overactive imagination, I expect. So tomorrow I don't want to see you, at least not here at the museum. You've earned a day off."

"You're not going to do something desperate, are you?"

I looked up, startled.

"Tomorrow, I mean."

"No, of course not. Tomorrow I'm taking your advice, and I'm going to be social. Football potluck at Mac's tavern."

Greg chuckled. "This town is an enigma to me."

"Me, too, which is why I love it."

oOo

On Sunday morning I slept in until Tuppence's whining at the door reached the urgent pitch I had learned to take seriously.

While Tuppence chased squirrels and reestablished her perimeter around the campsite, I prepared ingredients for my signature potluck contribution known as cheesy potatoes. I spooned the whole fattening conglomeration into a casserole dish and set it in the oven for a nice, low bake.

With a sweatshirt pulled on over my pajamas, I strolled to the river's edge. Large boulders lined the bank and provided a hard but ringside seat to enjoy the view. Tuppence clambered after me, tongue hanging, the white tip of her tail perked in the air.

High horsetail cirrus clouds feathered across the sky. Rain would come in a day or two. It was time. The seasonal changes were more dramatic, and somehow both faster and slower, than in the city—probably because I couldn't help but notice them now in my exposed living conditions, while they'd gone unheeded among the gray concrete barriers of the city.

Trees go from green to yellow and then to bare in a matter of days, pummeled by stiff gorge winds. If cold nights linger before the rains come, vine maples will highlight the deep-blue sky with flickering red-orange leaves—one of my countless favorite sights.

I inhaled the briny smell of freshwater algae and mud along with recently cut grass. Herb must have been out on the riding mower the day before. I hoped to have as much energy as he did when I was almost eighty.

When the rains arrived, Herb and Harriet would turn off the irrigation system. I always miss the nighttime tick-tick white noise of the sprinklers. I'll wake up in the wee hours because of the silence until I become accustomed to it, a sort of seasonal jet lag.

Then the storms come—raging wind and pelting rain that shudder my poor little trailer down to its jacks. I love those nights, provided I can sit in front of the fireplace and drink Earl Grey tea. Tuppence doesn't share my enthusiasm for eventful weather.

The timer in my pocket buzzed, and I reluctantly returned to the trailer. Bubbling cheesiness greeted me, prompting my stomach to growl. I took the casserole out of the oven and hurried to shower and dress.

With the hot dish nestled in an old, clean blanket, I drove to Mac's Sidetrack Tavern. The parking lot was filling up with the late-riser and after-church crowd.

I had been a bit shocked when I learned Mac hosted community potlucks at his tavern. But it all made sense when Pastor Mort explained the tavern was the only place in miles that had reliable NFL and college football coverage. Television reception is a tricky thing in the gorge. Mac wisely assessed that it's vital to his business, so he has satellite dishes from all the carriers stationed on his roof, antennas jabbed in every direction. He guarantees every single broadcast football game can be seen on one of his big screens.

Mac cordons off the stand-up bar at the far end of the tavern on Sundays to open up the rest of the large room for families. He doesn't have a license to serve food beyond peanuts, pretzels, and tortilla chips smothered in nacho cheese sauce from a #10 can, so everyone brings a hot dish to share and buys soft drinks, coffee, or lemonade to thank Mac for his hospitality. I'm not sure the arrangement is strictly legal, but liquor license inspectors are rare in these parts and don't work on Sundays anyway.

I pulled in beside the Levine family minivan. Pastor Mort was helping his wife, Sally, unload a Crock-Pot and cooler. Sally waved.

"Hey, Meredith," Pastor Mort said, sweating slightly. He's pudgy, and I know why. Sally's a great cook. "How've you been?"

"Good. Busy."

"I heard you got a shipment at the museum. When can we see the new exhibit?" Sally asked.

"Thursday."

"Wonderful! I'll be there with my class." Sally teaches kindergarten, an energetic jumble of five-year-olds.

I grinned. "I think you'll find it very educational."

I set my casserole on the designated table and found an empty seat next to Sheriff Marge in front of the Seattle Seahawks game.

Sheriff Marge was in uniform, but she's *always* in uniform. With only three deputies and herself to cover Sockeye County, she's never really off duty.

I can't tell if the bulletproof vest functions like a corset, lacing the sheriff's torso into that thick, tubular shape, or if it just adds several inches of armored padding around what's already there. Everything about Sheriff Marge is utilitarian.

"How's preserving the peace going?"

Sheriff Marge shifted her no-nonsense bulk in my direction. "Found a marijuana grow just off County Road 68. Booby trap mangled the leg of the deer hunter who stepped on it." She shook her head. "Makes me sick the grow workers got away. They would have been low-level, but maybe they could have led us to the ringleaders. This problem is getting worse in a hurry. It's so destructive—for people, plants, animals—everything."

She leaned back and sighed. "Other than that, a couple punks shoplifted a pack of cigarettes from Junction General. And a handful of DUIs, including one guy who knew he was too drunk to drive his truck but figured riding a quad on State Route 14 would be okay." She shrugged. "Status quo."

"I don't know how you do it."

"I watched Big John do it all those years. He always talked about investigations, asked what I thought about people and situations. I figured a couple decades of that was enough education to go on. Pays off, you know, knowing people."

I wondered what it would be like to always refer to my husband with an adjective in front of his name. Steely Dan, Pistol Pete, Fat Albert. Maybe you got used to it. Maybe it was like those Southern double names. Billy Bob. Bobby Ray. Big John. And by all reports, he'd been big—well over three hundred pounds. Made Sheriff Marge look like a debutante by comparison.

Sheriff's an elected position. Marge had been appointed to fill the role when her husband died of a heart attack midterm. She's run unopposed in every subsequent election.

"I saw you at the game—with Pete Sills," Sheriff Marge said.

I blew out a breath and rolled my eyes.

"Uh-huh." Sheriff Marge leveled gray eyes at me over the tops of silver-rimmed reading glasses. She doesn't bother with a beaded lanyard or even take the time to prop the glasses on the top of her head. She keeps them where she needs them and looks over them when she doesn't.

"Hi, Meredith. Great to see you." Mac leaned over the back of my chair, his callused hands weighing on my shoulders. "What can I get you to drink?"

From my vantage point, I had a rather disturbing view up his nostrils. It's obvious the man works with sawdust. I was glad I was wearing a high-necked T-shirt, otherwise he would have had an equally disturbing view down my cleavage.

"Arnold Palmer?"

"Sure thing for a pretty thing." He trotted toward the bar.

"Mm-hmm." Sheriff Marge grunted.

I sighed. "Yeah."

"You know what they say about hick towns. And I can say this, 'cause I'm from here."

"What?"

"The odds may be good, but the goods may be odd."

I screeched a very unladylike laugh before I was able to clamp a hand over my mouth. When I recovered, I asked, "What about you? Ever think about dating again?"

"Nope. Big John was my one-and-only. Besides, I'm too old and tired for that sort of thing. I'd rather bust meth-heads."

People shushed one another until the room quieted except for the shuffling of hungry children. Pastor Mort stood on his tiptoes between the main-dish and dessert tables.

"Welcome, folks. Good to see so many of you here. I'm going to thank the Lord for the meal, then you can line up on both sides of the tables to fill your plates. As usual, we let families with small children go first."

A little girl with blonde ringlet pigtails stood on a chair next to her seated dad, her arms around his neck. "That's me!"

Pastor Mort chuckled. "We should all come before God with the delightful hunger of children. He provides for us beyond measure." He bowed his head. "Lord God, thank You for this food and this fellowship. Thanks for taking care of us. Help us to seek You, Your truth, Your Word and the salvation You provided through Your Son when we deserve the opposite. Amen."

An orderly rush to the food tables ensued. I hung back with Sheriff Marge and enjoyed the scene. There's always more than enough food.

The women consider cooking a competitive sport, measuring success by how much of their entry is consumed. Casserole dishes scraped down to the ceramic glaze score a 10.0.

"Here you are." Mac slid into a chair beside me and handed me a tall glass of iced tea mixed with lemonade, dripping with condensation. He'd stuck an umbrella toothpick in a lemon wedge and floated it in the drink.

"Oh, thanks. It's very—tropical."

"Hey, I thought I saw Bard Joseph the other day, driving through town," Mac said.

Sheriff Marge's eyebrows shot up.

Mac shrugged. "I was just surprised. That's all."

"How about some coffee? Black." Sheriff Marge scowled.

"Comin' up." Mac stood and walked back to the bar.

"Troublemaker?" I asked.

"Hmm?" Sheriff Marge wasn't paying attention.

"The person Mac just mentioned. I don't know any Josephs."

"Wealthiest family—what's left of it—in the county. Land-rich, anyway. Maybe not cash-rich. But you wouldn't have met them. A bit reclusive."

Sheriff Marge and I got in line and filled our plates from steaming Crock-Pots and casserole dishes in quilted cozies. I'd left my embarrassing old blanket in the truck and let my casserole sit naked on the table.

I have a rule not to eat my own food at potlucks. That would be like stuffing the ballot box. Plus, it's important to sample all the other goodness available. A couple of times unpleasant surprises have marred my experience, but it's still a risk I gladly take. I wedged a slice of pear pie with a crumble pecan topping next to scoops of beef stroganoff and rice pilaf.

Sheriff Marge stopped to talk to a family of migrant workers, some of the last remaining since the apple harvest had wrapped up a week or so ago.

I spied a single empty chair between the Levines and another church family with a whole passel of little kids. I knew I was being rude to Mac, but he has a tendency to overinterpret even a whiff of encouragement—or rather he has an ability to find encouragement in innocuous actions or words that completely baffles me.

I leaned across the table toward Sally. "Have you ever thought about putting together a recipe book as a community fundraiser? I think it would be a bestseller in the museum gift shop." Certainly better than those dusty refrigerator magnets.

Sally's eyebrows arched. "A couple other people have mentioned the same thing, but I wouldn't know where to start."

"I could help get quotes on printing if you did the recipe collecting."

The mom of the young family on my other side raised her fork to hold her place in the conversation while she finished chewing. "I could do the page layouts and covers. I worked for an ad firm before I married Paul. I'm a little rusty, but I still have the software. I could work on it during nap times."

I recognized Paul as a grain inspector from the port. He was busy trying to spoon what looked like pureed beets into a chubby baby's clamped mouth.

"I could put an announcement in the church bulletin, an APB for recipes," Sally said.

"APB?" Sheriff Marge's antenna picked that up through thirty feet of mingled conversations, and she bustled over.

Sally laughed. "For your caramel brownie bar recipe." She filled in until Sheriff Marge nodded.

"Ah." Sheriff Marge stabbed a stout finger at the gooey golden mound on her plate. "Then Meredith will have to share her recipe for these cheesy potatoes."

"Deal."

The Seahawks lost, as usual. The subdued crowd stacked folding chairs and wiped down tables. I collected my empty casserole dish. It was so clean it looked like Tuppence had had a go at it, except not as slimy. Perfect score.

I joined the throng of adults assembling the remains of tableware and sleepy children and packing them into cars for the ride home.

Pastor Mort ambled out with me. "We'd love to see you at church sometime."

He wasn't just saying that because he was supposed to. The Levines really mean it; they're good people. I couldn't remember the last time I'd been to church—a lifetime, a career, and a fiancé ago. Churchgoing would probably do me some good, maybe make me less of the loner Greg and Pete had so helpfully pointed out I was becoming lately.

"I'd like that, too." I smiled at Pastor Mort. "And tell Sally to call me when she's ready to brainstorm about the cookbook."

ooo

On Monday, a free day all to myself, I layered jeans and a thermal long-sleeved T-shirt over silk long johns. I pulled on wool socks and hiking boots, and found my fingerless mitts and flannel-lined canvas field coat.

After loading a backpack with a few sandwiches and several bottles of water, I called to my ecstatic hound and flopped a blanket on the passenger side of the bench seat so she could curl up on it. It was way too cold to drive with the windows down, so Tuppence would have to make do with leaving nose smears on the glass.

I drove east on State Route 14 to Lupine, the county seat and closest town substantial enough to have a hardware/household goods/craft supply/drugstore. I took Greg's suggestion and bought a bright-yellow plastic potty chair. No pink or blue versions here, just utilitarian yellow.

Then I kept driving, up the gorge toward the empty expanse of rolling latte-tan hills with the horizon rimmed by gleaming white phalanxes of wind turbines. A thick drizzle misted the windshield. The truck was old enough not to have intermittent windshield wipers, so I flicked the lever every minute or so.

The gray Columbia churned with short whitecaps casting off flicks of spray. The river was a bit agitated. I wondered if salmon and sturgeon were hunkered at the bottom, sitting this one out.

I pulled into the empty gravel parking lot at a Lewis and Clark heritage trail marker. "Ready to get wet?"

Tuppence thumped her tail once and licked her chops. She was so ready she was salivating.

She had definitely been neglected the past couple months. With winter coming fast, we had to get our exploring in while we could, rain or no.

I put on my hat and opened the door, my booted feet landing in a puddle. Tuppence scrambled over and jumped into the same puddle. Had to start somewhere.

I flipped my coat collar up and inhaled deeply, grinning. This was the life. Who would have believed, two years ago, that I would go hiking in the rain without another human being in sight, and love it?

We set off cross-country. Hard to get lost with nothing blocking the view of the biggest landmark—water-mark—around. Even better, the landmark was directional. Downstream was west, toward home, and eventually, if you kept going, Astoria and the Pacific Ocean.

The white tip of Tuppence's tail waved like a flag marker in the tall grass. I forged a straight path across Tuppence's zigzags. The grass would green up with just a few rainy days like this one, and the hills would magically transform into a land resembling the Emerald Isle.

I huffed up a hillock, my thighs and calves burning by the time I reached the top—the effect of too many late-night grilled cheese sandwiches.

I spun slowly to take in the entire panorama. Squalls were coming up from the southwest. Under the thick overcast layer, tightfisted black cloud knots rushed low over the hills, trailing torrential downpours like veils. Several tempestuous, runaway brides on the Oregon side. There but for the grace of God. I shook my head, grinning again. It's good to be free.

Tuppence poked her nose down a hole and sneezed.

"Not at home? Or they didn't invite you in?"

Tuppence glanced at me over her shoulder, then started to dig.

"Come on, girl, leave them alone. Come on." I whistled and trekked up the next incline.

Four hours later we made our way back. Tuppence had definitely lost her zip. My legs wobbled. I'd sleep hard that night and feel it the next day, but it had been so worth it.

I scanned the river, soaking its wild frothiness into my soul—inhaling it. Fresh rain meeting the well-traveled water in the river tingled my senses. The Columbia held secrets—deep ones, old ones, plus new ones in the flotsam. Time and mystery flowed in its component molecules. Long ago the local tribes had buried their ancestors on islands in the river.

We climbed into the truck, and I pulled off my outer layers. We stank in tandem of wet dog and sweat-soaked wool, and steamed up the windows immediately. I shared the last sandwich with Tuppence while the defroster blasted.

I swung through Caffè-a-Go-Go on the way home in an attempt to keep myself awake. My rubbery body gelled into the seat contours. My hands felt like ten-pound weights, my fingertips barely able to keep them in place on the steering wheel. Tuppence snored.

As I passed the Imogene Museum a mile from home, Pete's concern about Ford niggled at me. The small cabin was barely visible through the trees. *I should check on him,* I thought, *when I'm more alert.*

CHAPTER 5

Late Tuesday afternoon Mac backed his rusty step van up to the museum's side door, lurching slowly as Ford gave him conflicting hand signals.

I yelled, "Stop!" at the last moment—to save a large terra-cotta flowerpot and to prevent yet another dent in Mac's bumper.

Ford was so excited that spittle clung to his lips when he spoke. "Nice and easy. Nice and easy." He unlatched the van's roll-up door and gave it a push.

Ford was in his element when I asked him to lend his expertise in the form of strong back and shoulders to shove display cases into place. And Mac was so good with Ford—they were drinking buddies to the extent that teetotaler Ford enjoyed Dr Pepper while Mac swigged an amber ale or two during *SportsCenter* at the Sidetrack.

Mac slammed the driver's door closed and bounded around to the back. His legs must be made of springs. I quickly squashed the fleeting image of what he might look like in shorts. Sometimes my subconscious scares me.

Mac was bundled in a heavy flannel jacket with a watch cap pulled tight over his head. The first frost had come overnight, and the temperature hovered barely above freezing now—the warmest part of the day. Mac's sparse mushroom-beige hair doesn't show up well on his balding scalp, so he shaves it off and has taken to wearing hats. The problem is, the hats emphasize the fact that something's not quite symmetrical about his head.

Mac's like those puzzles in kiddie activity books where there's a lineup of the same person drawn five times and you're supposed to find the identical two by discovering slight variances in the others—a belt buckle off-center or shoes different colors or freckles versus no freckles. Mac's eliminating feature is a missing left earlobe. Same incident when he lost his left pinkie finger down to the first knuckle.

I understand how fingers can get in the way when one is operating a table saw, but an earlobe? Still a mystery. Not that Mac hadn't related the episode in great detail the first time we met. After a quick handshake, he said, "I suppose you noticed I'm missing an earlobe," and then he didn't shut up for half an hour.

But the focus of his story was more on the search for and final recovery of the earlobe from an open polyurethane container two days later. I hadn't had the stomach to ask for more information. Unfortunately, Mac missed out on the stoicism stereotypical of Scotsmen.

His chin and lower jaw were covered with scraggly red blotches as if he'd developed rosacea since Sunday. I stepped next to him to examine the cases in the back of the van and realized it was new beard growth. I know a couple of men whose beards come in a different color from their head hair, but the red surprised me.

"Hey, I missed saying good-bye to you on Sunday," Mac said.

I thought back to my quick escape in the midst of the crowd. I hated to admit it had been intentional, so I changed the subject. "Growing a beard?"

"Yeah," he grunted. He turned to look at me. He has blue eyes, not sapphire-blue like Pete's, but pale, washed-out blue, like their vitality had leaked and left pinprick pupils behind. "Starting to get cold. Figured if I had hair on my face to keep me warm I wouldn't have to heat the workshop so much. Save some money."

Mac and Ford wheeled the first case down the ramp.

"Have you been going without sleep to work on these cases?" I asked.

I waited for the answer while Mac and Ford tipped the second case up and wedged dollies underneath.

"What? Nah."

I was pretty sure he was lying.

"I wanted to ask you Sunday. I could always shave it off." He looked at me hopefully, his warm breath coming in spurts on the cold air. "Pete Sills has a beard."

Ah.

I held the door open for them and wondered if Mac realized how transparent he was. I was also pretty sure Pete Sills didn't care one iota what other people thought of his appearance, and his beard was most certainly not for my benefit. If he'd asked, I would have told him I preferred clean-shaven men. Scratchy neck nuzzles aren't my thing.

"Makes sense to me," I answered. "What about your hands, though? When my hands are cold, I get clumsier. You'll want to keep your remaining digits intact."

Mac flushed brightly like the latent redhead he apparently is and said, "I have *all* of my digits."

I shook my head. "Digits are fingers and toes."

"Oh. In that case, I have nineteen and a half out of twenty."

I left him doing the math and ducked down a hall and around a corner to grab a transit cart of chamber pots. I wheeled it into the freight elevator beside the first two cases.

On the way up, Mac said, "So, on a scale from one to ten, I'm a nine point five." He elbowed me and winked. "Not bad, eh?"

I tried to laugh it off, but the sound came out more like the noise old Amos Stanley makes when he hawks loogies and spits on the sidewalk in front of God and everyone, especially ladies. He also clears a path through the earwax by inserting an index finger and waggling it vigorously, but that's beside the point. At least old Amos hadn't asked me out yet.

"Nice and easy," Ford crooned.

The guys wrangled the cases into place and left to get the others while I started arranging chamber pots. I couldn't remember the exact sequence, so I dashed upstairs for the description cards, my leg muscles reminding me of the previous day's long hike.

The phone rang just as I opened my office door.

"Hello?" I answered, breathless.

The red message light was flashing. Since when did I get messages on my work line?

"Ah, we speak at last."

"Excuse me?"

"This is Dr. Clyde Elroy. I believe you are supervising the internship of one of my students, Greg Boykin?"

"Yes, I am." *What of it,* I wanted to say, but held my tongue for Greg's sake. His adviser sounded pinched and nasal, like he was looking down his nose just to talk on the phone.

"I wanted to know if you're requiring overtime of Greg without my permission."

And Greg thought I should meet this guy. Huh.

"Well, he did come early on Thursday, but that was because he wanted to. We received a new collection—"

Dr. Elroy cut me off. "I mean yesterday and so far today."

"No, I gave Greg Sunday off since he worked so hard—"

"Do you know where he is?"

I gritted my teeth. His rudeness was off the chart. "He should be in Corvallis, attending classes as usual."

"He missed his weekly four o'clock meeting with me yesterday, and he's not answering his phone."

Maybe he got fed up with your snobbishness, I thought.

"I checked with his other professors. He did not attend his classes yesterday or today."

Okay, that was a problem. "As far as I know, he left here on Sunday, possibly even earlier than normal, since he had no commitments here at the museum."

"And as far as I know, he never arrived here," Dr. Elroy answered.

"Have you called his parents, his friends?"

"His mother is next on my list. I didn't want to worry her unnecessarily."

I exhaled. "I see. While you do that, I'll call the lady he rents a room from to see if she knows what time he left."

"Thank you." Dr. Elroy clicked off.

My knees wobbled, and I dropped into the chair. Greg was nothing if not reliable. The thought of his Prius mangled against a concrete barrier along I-5 made my stomach cramp.

"Please, no. Please, no," I whispered as I flipped through the county white pages booklet looking for Betty Jenkins's number. Hoping the *E* stood for Elizabeth, I dialed. The other options were *T* and *O*.

"Hello?" A sweet, light voice answered.

"Betty? Mrs. Jenkins? This is Meredith Morehouse from the Imogene Museum. Is Greg still there?"

"Oh, no, honey. He left early on Sunday, right after—"

Her last few words were drowned out by loud rumbling that had to be a freight train. We waited a solid two minutes until it was quiet enough to speak again.

"What did you say?" I asked.

"Right after breakfast. He's such a kind boy. He helped me wash the dishes, then left in that tiny car of his."

"Did he say where he was going?"

"Oh, no, dear. He always goes back to school on Sundays."

"Did he leave anything in his room, as though he was going out but would come back?"

"I don't know about that. I told him he could leave his things here during the week. No sense in packing them away every time, since he's my only lodger. I clean his room, but I don't disturb his things. He doesn't usually leave much."

"Oh, I know," I said. "You take good care of him. His professor called. It seems Greg didn't make it back to school on Sunday. Did he say anything to you about stopping along the way home?"

"Oh dear. No. I'm afraid I rattled on about this and that, and he didn't say much at all."

"Do you remember anything he did say?"

"Just polite things like, 'Let me help you with that.'"

"All right. I need to go now, Mrs. Jenkins. I'll call you if I hear anything."

"Okay, sweetie. Oh dear."

I found Dr. Elroy's phone number from caller ID and dialed. "His landlady says he left Sunday morning right after breakfast."

"His mother hasn't heard from him since last week. And then she panicked on me." Dr. Elroy sighed. "Obviously I don't have his friends' phone numbers. I will notify the Oregon State Police. They have an office here on campus, and they could check his apartment."

I nodded, then remembered he couldn't see me. "Yeah, that sounds good. I'll call the county sheriff. She's a friend." I took a deep breath. "We'll find him."

"Greg is one of my best students, you know."

"I'm not surprised." I liked Dr. Elroy better now. After giving him my cell phone number, I hung up and called Sheriff Marge.

"Where are you?" Sheriff Marge asked when I finished explaining.

"At the museum."

"Stay there. I'm going to put out a missing person report, then I'll pick you up. We need to have a look at his room at Betty's."

My stomach was doing the cramping thing again. Sheriff Marge's voice was all business, which meant she thought it was serious.

"Greg's Prius is silver, isn't it?" Sheriff Marge asked.

"Yes."

"Know the license number?"

"No." The word strangled my throat.

"I'll check with OSP."

I was still staring at my phone when Mac tapped softly on the open door.

"We have all the cases in place," he said. "Want to come inspect?"

"Oh, Mac." My eyes welled up, and I squeezed them shut. I hate crying. It would be even worse in front of Mac. "Greg's missing."

"You sure?"

I nodded.

"Aw, he's probably off cavorting. He's a young guy." Mac said it like he had outgrown that distant phase of his history. He patted my shoulder.

I took a deep breath and followed Mac downstairs to the exhibit bedroom where Ford was dusting the new cases with his sleeve.

"As usual, Mac, they're wonderful."

"I rigged the lights in all the cases to one switch." Mac pointed at Ford, who flipped the switch and grinned.

"Perfect. Thank you." I tried to smile. "I have to go with Sheriff Marge now, so I'm going to lock the room until I have a chance to arrange the exhibit. Sorry to cut it short, guys."

"Sheriff Marge goin' to arrest you?" Ford asked.

"No, we're looking for Greg."

"Uh-oh." Ford said. Having the sheriff looking for you was a bad thing in his world.

"Yeah," I whispered.

Mac watched me lock up, then squeezed my elbow. "There are lots of reasons Greg might not be in contact for a few days," he said. "He'll turn up. But if Sheriff Marge wants to launch a search, tell her I'm in."

"Thanks, Mac."

I remembered the flashing light on my phone and ran back to my office. All the messages, four of them, were from Dr. Elroy, ranging from "please call me at your convenience" to "call me immediately." He was more worried than he had let on. I knew every minute counted with missing persons. And if Greg had been in an accident on Sunday, we were already into day three—way past counting hours, let alone minutes.

CHAPTER 6

I paced along the sidewalk in front of the museum, mind racing. Maybe Mac was right—maybe Greg was on a spontaneous road trip. But he would never miss an appointment with his adviser without at least calling to cancel ahead of time. Greg was way too responsible to forget a regular appointment. So he was sick, or injured, or—no, I refused to consider worse possibilities.

A dirty white Ford Explorer with a light bar on top and county logo on the front doors zipped down the tree-lined driveway and charged toward the museum. Sheriff Marge skidded to a stop and leaned over to pop open the passenger door. The SUV's suspension was shot, and it was still bouncing as I climbed in and buckled up.

"Good news—no accidents reported involving a Toyota Prius since Thursday on the main route between here and Corvallis," Sheriff Marge announced. "One in Madras and one outside Spokane, neither silver."

"What about nonmain routes?"

"Nothing reported. If he was in a single-car accident and went off the road into a ravine where no one driving by can see him, well, then—" Sheriff Marge didn't finish the thought. "We can't search everywhere. It's nearly two hundred miles. Which is why we're going to look through his stuff for clues as to where he might have gone." She gunned the Explorer onto the highway. "You with me on this, Meredith? I need your brain in gear."

"Yeah. Yeah, I'm okay." I balled my right hand into a fist and clamped my left hand around it to keep them from trembling.

If my nerves had been taut when I got in the Explorer, they were a fraction away from fraying through when Sheriff Marge slammed on the brakes in Betty Jenkins's potholed driveway.

Something about Sheriff Marge's girth had kept her firmly grounded behind the wheel, but I had been slung from side to side against the lap belt as Sheriff Marge cornered going fifty and jounced the old battleship over roads that hadn't seen a paving crew in a decade. I actually rose off the seat at one point and felt my hair brush the roof. I braced a foot against the dashboard and clung to the door handle. If the county couldn't afford a new four-wheel-drive police cruiser, it should at least install five-point harnesses in the ones it had.

Betty came rushing out at the sound of crunching gravel and stood swathed in a ruffled floral apron, wringing her hands. "Did you find him?" Her voice warbled.

I clung to the side mirror for a few seconds to steady my legs before venturing toward Betty's porch. Solid ground had never felt so good. I'd even forgotten about Greg for a few minutes, but at first sight of Betty, worry, bordering on panic, flooded over me.

"Not yet," Sheriff Marge answered, "but we will. We need to look at his room."

"Wasn't he going home?"

"Could be. But we have to think about all the possibilities."

I caught Betty under the elbow as her knees sagged, and helped her onto the creaking porch swing.

"Oh dear," the old lady murmured. "I talked and talked Sunday morning to cheer him up. Maybe he would have told me what he was planning if I hadn't been such a chatterbox."

Sheriff Marge squatted beside the swing. "Was Greg sad, depressed?"

Betty nodded, her silver ponytail bobbing against her back. "Sad. Anxious maybe. That young lady he's fond of—"

"Angie," I said.

"Yes, that's the one," Betty said. "He was worried she may have found someone else, someone—I forget—some foreign name."

"Lorenzo." The word came out like a snarl. I even startled myself. The other women looked at me in surprise. "But they're in Turkey. He can't drive there."

"I think he felt like he disappointed his girlfriend, wasn't enough to impress her," Betty added. "I tried to tell him that sometimes it's best if things don't work out the way you want, because sometimes what you want isn't best, but you can't tell right away. I told him all about my first engagement, which broke off when I met Roland." Betty dabbed her eyes. "Oh dear. Maybe that wasn't helpful."

Sheriff Marge said, "I could really use a cup of coffee."

"Oh, how thoughtless of me! Of course." Betty scurried into the kitchen.

Sheriff Marge and I followed her into the worn but cozy little room crowded with a dinette table and four chairs from the 1950s. Cracked linoleum the color of speckled parchment covered the floor. Narrow counters flanked the walls, and an ancient refrigerator wheezed in the far corner. Betty filled an aluminum percolator-style electric coffeepot at a deep farm sink that my old friends would have fought for the chance to put in their own designer homes.

"Greg's room is down the hall, Betty?" Sheriff Marge asked, already sidling into the narrow opening.

"Second door on the right," Betty called.

The eyes of Betty's extended family followed me from their picture frames jam-packed on the hallway walls. I had to be careful not to brush any of them with my shoulders. I stepped into the cramped bedroom and peered around Sheriff Marge.

A narrow bed with a crocheted coverlet cut the room in half. It looked shorter than normal. Greg probably had to sleep with his knees pulled up. A small desk holding an alarm clock and lamp fit between the bed and the far wall. A metal folding chair was pushed against the wall in front of the desk, a pile of books on the seat.

Across from the foot of the bed, a maple dresser sported an antique washbasin and pitcher. I leaned in to examine them. The transferware design might have been the same as on one of the chamber pots in the new collection. A matched set. Maybe Betty would loan them to the museum.

I caught my reflection in the mirror above the dresser—my face was ghastly pale—and my mind jerked back to the reason I was in Greg's room.

Sheriff Marge pulled on the glass knob of the slender closet door. A handful of empty wire hangers hung on the rod. A couple of plastic tubs on the floor held what looked like Betty's stash of hand-knit baby sweaters, hats, and blankets, ready for the next several newborns in town.

I wriggled around to the desk. The books on the chair were mine, the ones Greg had borrowed. I moved them to the bed and sat on the chair.

I opened the right-hand desk drawer and came up with a number two pencil and a half-inch stack of standard-ruled notebook paper. The left drawer held a stapler, a couple of petrified rubber bands, and a small 1998 calendar from Brown's Insurance Agency.

Bending in half, I looked under the desk. Yep, an outlet. Greg would have done all of his work on his laptop. The garbage can was empty.

The room's bleakness settled on my shoulders. Greg didn't really live here, hadn't left any of himself here. I wondered at his nomadic life, the temporary shelters. And with his girlfriend out of the country, he had to be lonely. Where would a lonely, single young guy go?

My eyes widened, and I impulsively shook my head to delete the unbidden thought that had popped into my mind. Greg's character was impeccable, and he was clearly smitten with Angie. He wouldn't keep additional female companionship on the side. I gritted my teeth. I hate when my history rears up to taint others. Not every man is like my ex-fiancé.

The floor began to vibrate. Within seconds the deafening roar of a freight train filled the house. Sheriff Marge worked the strings to pull up the Venetian blinds on the high window above the bed. We could see the top foot or so of the loaded coal cars flashing by. The tracks were probably fifty feet away, but they might as well have been in the room.

Sheriff Marge pulled out dresser drawers, stacking them neatly on the bed. They, as well as the interior cavity of the dresser, were empty. There were no manila envelopes taped to the undersides of the drawers, not that I'd expected any. Greg wasn't a spy or a mob informer; he was a graduate student.

If Greg had revealed his worries about his fickle girlfriend to Betty, then he wasn't a secret-keeper, either. That surprised me. He'd been reluctant to tell me about Angie. Maybe he trusted Betty more than he trusted me. I frowned. Had I let him down? Probably. Too absorbed in ancient artifacts to pay much attention to the people right in front of me. I wished I had the lunch at the Burger Basket to do over—really, all of Friday and Saturday, knowing now it was the last time I'd seen him.

Betty appeared in the doorway with a tray of coffee mugs. She looked like the quintessential grandmother. Anyone would trust her, including Greg. She slid the tray onto the dresser next to the washbasin and watched us replace the drawers. The train whistle blasted at an intersection a mile away, and the rumble faded.

"When did you clean the room, Betty?" Sheriff Marge lifted the edge of the mattress.

"Sunday, after church. I like to do it right away. Oh dear."

"It's all right, Betty. You had no way of knowing."

"Was there anything in the garbage can?" I felt bad for asking. Poor Betty—she was being subjected to a housekeeping inspection in her own home.

"A few scraps of paper, some tissues," Betty answered.

"When's your garbage pickup?" Sheriff Marge asked.

"Tomorrow. But the papers are gone. I burned them in the wood stove, like I usually do. No sense clogging the landfill with that. Oh dear." Betty sat on the bed and covered her face with her hands.

I rubbed Betty's shoulder. "It probably doesn't matter. I expect Greg used his laptop for important things."

"Oh, yes." Betty perked up. "That's what he always did. Sat at the desk and typed on his computer, for hours and hours. Sometimes he would chat with me in the living room, but mostly he studied."

Sheriff Marge drained her coffee cup. "Thanks, Betty. If you think of anything else he said, anything out of the ordinary, let me know."

Betty stood on the porch and watched us leave.

"What now?" I asked.

"For you, nothing. Stay near your phone."

"What do you mean?"

Sheriff Marge eyed me over the tops of her glasses as we bounced along. "My deputies and I will be driving the county roads—State Route 14 and all others generally heading west—keeping a lookout for places where Greg might have gone off the road. WSP and OSP have their eyes peeled on the rest of his expected route." She turned on the blinker and slowed. "Until we have a reported sighting with a more specific location, that's all we can do. The Portland TV stations will be running his photo and the Prius's license number on the news tonight."

I stewed in silence. I didn't like it, but I wasn't going to argue with Sheriff Marge, either, since I didn't have any better ideas.

Sheriff Marge dropped me off in front of the museum. Lindsay was behind the gift-shop counter when I entered.

"Did you find him?" Lindsay had twirled knots in her long blonde hair.

"Not yet. Did he say anything to you Friday at the game—or any other time—about plans he had for going somewhere?"

"No, just football talk." Lindsay sniffed. Her brown eyes were puffy and pink-rimmed. Had she been crying about Greg?

"I'm sure they'll find him, Lindsay. Sheriff Marge has everyone on it, searching the roads."

Lindsay nodded and swiped at the glass case with her cleaning rag.

"There's something else, isn't there?"

Uh-oh, tears. I wanted to dissolve alongside Lindsay, but I had to hold myself together, had to be the responsible one. And think clearly.

"You want to tell me?"

"You know when Greg said those nice things about me, about how I can explain football?"

"Uh-huh."

"Well, after that, after a touchdown, I hugged him. I was just so excited and happy and jumping up and down, and I hugged him. Mark saw it, and we had a big fight. He doesn't understand that when I'm happy I hug people. I didn't mean anything by it." Lindsay wiped her nose on the back of her hand. "Do you think Mark did something to Greg? He was really angry."

"When was the last time you saw Mark?"

"Saturday morning, when we had the fight."

"Don't worry about it, okay? I like that you're an indiscriminate hugger. It's one of my favorite things about you."

"Really?"

"Really. And if Mark can't figure out how wonderful you are, you should ditch him."

Lindsay managed an uncomfortable half smile. "You don't think Greg is into drugs, do you?"

My mouth dropped open. "What makes you say that?"

"A guy I know, Bard Joseph—he was a few years ahead of me in high school—got into drugs and disappeared. I heard he's back in town.

But he's been gone for a long time. Everybody says his disappearance devastated his dad." Lindsay chewed her lip. "And sometimes Mark—well, I know he smokes pot sometimes."

"Lindsay. Why are you going out with him?"

Lindsay shrunk into her shoulders, her face apprehensive.

"Look, I don't think Greg's ever had anything to do with drugs. And you need to take care of yourself, kiddo. It doesn't sound like Mark's good for you."

"I know." Lindsay sighed.

I stomped up the stairs to my office, frustrated with Lindsay for not seeing her own worth. But maybe gullible, naive Lindsay had more backbone—sticking it out and hoping for the best. I'd fled from the life surrounding my ex-fiancé precisely because I hadn't had the backbone to face all my family and friends and their expectations. With my track record, I certainly wasn't qualified to offer relationship advice.

I dialed Sheriff Marge and filled her in on Lindsay's worries.

"Huh. Those Mason kids are not exactly the cream of the crop. Mark's older brother, also a good quarterback, is serving time for possession and distribution. His sister is probably using, too, but she's not my problem since she skipped to Las Vegas for a quickie wedding and stayed there." Brakes squealed in the background. "I'll drop by the Mason farm. Probably find a few baggies of dope, but I'd be real surprised if Mark actually assaulted Greg. He's mostly hot air."

Next I called Dr. Elroy and left a message when he didn't answer.

I stood at the window, watching the Columbia flow by, serene and gray-green today. Was Greg also staring at the Columbia right now? I wished the river were telepathic, taking my thoughts to him, or bringing his to me.

"Where are you?" I whispered.

My phone rang.

"Meredith, this is Clyde Elroy. And please, call me Clyde. Your message was so formal. I have no news, either. I went with an OSP trooper to check Greg's apartment. He wasn't there, and everything looked normal. Most of his neighbors weren't home, but one girl did say she saw him leaving on Thursday, about midafternoon."

"That fits with when he arrived. We worked here at the museum for a few hours Thursday night."

Clyde sighed. "OSP says the only thing we can do now is hope the news segments tonight turn up valid tips. The Eugene station is going to air it, too."

"That's pretty much what Sheriff Marge told me."

"I'm thinking about coming your way. I can't stand sitting around here doing nothing. And since he was last seen up there—well, am I crazy?"

"No. I'd feel the same way. I should warn you, though—there isn't a motel within forty miles."

"I've already been searching the Internet. There are some decent places to stay in The Dalles."

"I'll be here at the museum tomorrow. You know where it is?"

"Yeah, Google Maps. See you."

I returned to the window. A couple of hours of daylight left. I didn't care what Sheriff Marge said—doing nothing was just not an option.

CHAPTER 7

I hurried home and opened the truck's passenger door for Tuppence. The dog scrambled in and thumped her tail on the seat while I cranked down the window.

"Use that nose of yours, old girl. If you smell Greg, let me know."

Tuppence's yawn ended in a whine.

We drove west on State Route 14 with freezing wind barreling in the open windows. What other route would Greg have taken? I slowed before every drop-off, checking for tire tracks in the gravel at the edge of the pavement and fresh scrapes on guardrails. All the roadside brushy growth looked intact. Tuppence snorted and sneezed into the wind, her ears flapping back.

I love the peace and solitude of driving—it helps me think. The easy rhythm of guardrail posts and the dashed yellow line calmed my swirling thoughts, although worry still weighed heavily.

I had been on only one road trip as a child, to my stepfather Alex's law-school reunion in Michigan. I'd sprawled in the backseat and spent the miles reading and drawing, separated from the tension between

Mom and Alex in the front seats. I knew better than to comment on landmarks and tourist signs we passed. Keep quiet. Be invisible.

Not that my mother and stepfather ever actually fight. No shouting or slamming of doors, because that isn't appropriate. And appropriateness is the standard by which they measure their lives. What would other people think?

I didn't realize it then, but appropriateness is usually the source of tension in their marriage. *You're not going to wear that dress to the fundraiser, are you? It's too short. Your gray's showing. Get your hair done before Senator Schmidt comes for dinner.*

And Mom has complaints as well. *You monopolized Mattie Donald over cocktails last night. It was all I could do to keep her husband from making a scene. If you keep playing golf with Ralph DiMarco, the bar association will think you're on his other payroll, too.*

What would other people think? What was Greg thinking? He was careful and precise in his research, so that must carry over into his everyday life. He wouldn't do anything rash or stupid. It had to be an accident. Maybe he was in a hospital right now. Maybe he had amnesia.

I kneaded the muscles in the back of my neck. Sheriff Marge would have checked the hospitals. Our best chance was the televised announcement tonight. Someone must have seen Greg.

I drove until dusk, coming closer and closer to real civilization and more drivers frustrated by my varying speeds. I got honked at more than once. When a black BMW tailgated and then passed, the angry driver flipping me off with one hand while pressing a cell phone to his ear with the other, I decided to turn around. My teeth chattered, and the rearview mirror showed that my lips were the purplish-blue color of a deep bruise. Tuppence curled on the seat with her nose tucked inside her haunch.

"Had enough, old girl?"

She blinked.

I took the next exit and stopped to roll up the windows.

We covered ground on the way home much faster. I pulled into Junction General's gravel parking lot. Metal bells clanked against the glass door as I pushed it open.

Gloria turned from where she'd been stocking cigarettes behind the counter. "Hey, Meredith. You look windblown."

"Been driving State Route 14, hoping for a sign of Greg."

Gloria nodded. "You and everyone else."

"Everyone else?"

"Law enforcement, anyway. I've had two sheriff's deputies and a state trooper stop in this afternoon, asking if I'd seen him. Mac asked, too. Sheriff Marge called."

"So you didn't see Greg, then? I thought maybe he'd stopped for gas or something."

Gloria shook her head. "He probably only has to fill that Prius up once a month."

"Oh, right." I looked around the store absently, trying to remember why I'd stopped.

"You need dog food?" Gloria asked.

"What? Oh, no. People food."

"The heat-and-serve stuff is in the freezer at the back."

That grated on me. Did I look like I couldn't cook?

Maybe Gloria was right. Not tonight.

I found individually wrapped bean-and-cheese burritos and bought two. Enough heavy carbs and fat to send me straight into a comatose slumber. Something to temporarily stifle the dull throb of worry.

Back in the RV, I nuked the burritos and checked my e-mail, hoping for a note from Greg. "Hey, I decided to go exploring. Here are some great photos I took of ____."

Nope. Greg didn't do that sort of thing. Come to think of it, he almost never e-mailed me. He was a texting man. I was grasping at anything, nothing, and no longer thinking straight.

The phone rang.

"I checked on the Mason boy," Sheriff Marge said. "Got an invitation from a college scout on Friday night to visit U-Dub, so he and his dad drove up to Seattle on Saturday and stayed the weekend."

"He was here on Saturday, arguing with Lindsay."

"Yeah, in the morning. They left right after. His mom's upset. She likes Lindsay. No remorse from the boy."

"Any other leads?"

"The TV tips are starting to come in, and we're sorting through them. Everything from a sighting at a gas station in Yreka to an alien vaporization right before the witness's eyes."

"Anything valid? Yreka's not too far."

"It's two hundred and fifty miles past Corvallis. We're focusing on our corridor, and state troopers are already out checking on a few tips. I'll keep you updated. Get some sleep."

The first bite of burrito turned to gummy paste in my mouth, reminding me of the flour-and-water concoction Mom made when I was little and wanted to glue stuff. Edible, nontoxic, and relatively easy to clean up. All it really needed to do was outlast my four-year-old attention span.

Which the burrito succeeded at as well—my appetite vanished. I dropped the burrito on the floor for Tuppence, who nosed it but didn't sample.

I slid into bed, fully clothed and cradling the phone, just in case.

CHAPTER 8

I awoke to the patter of rain, big fat blops that collected on tree branches overhead, then splatted on the fiberglass roof. My eyelids were glued shut with the crusty eye gunk that happens when I don't sleep normal hours like a normal person. I rubbed them open and peered at the clock—5:37 in red numbers. I exchanged the previous day's clothes for a comfortable old sweat suit. Maybe if I exercised I could get rid of the fitful nervous energy that made my limbs twitch.

Tuppence stood at the threshold for a minute watching the rain, then opted to stay inside and continue her beauty sleep. So much for faithful companionship.

I started off at a slow trot, counting strides between the pools of light cast by the lampposts spaced every third campsite. The drizzle quickly coated my face and neck with a sheen that wasn't yet sweat, but exertion kept my skin from feeling clammy. When was the last time I had gone for a run?

Hikes are good; running is bad. I remembered this after about a quarter mile when my side cramped and my sinuses ached from inhaling cold air. I walked back to the RV, shivering as I cooled down. Pathetic.

A steaming shower revived me. Plus coffee.

I decided to direct my energy toward making the chamber pot exhibit shine, as a tribute to Greg, and drove to the museum. Lindsay found me in the display bedroom a few hours later, dust-streaked and disheveled but making progress.

"Any news?" Lindsay didn't look like she'd slept much, either.

"No. Except you don't have to worry about Mark. He was at the University of Washington after you fought Saturday and all day Sunday, so he couldn't have done anything to Greg."

"Good riddance," Lindsay muttered.

"Really?"

"Yeah, I've been thinking about what you said, and about what Greg said. Washington State has a sports-management program that includes broadcasting. There are all kinds of options—marketing, working with Boys & Girls Clubs and youth teams, public relations. That would be so cool."

"You'd be perfect. Sounds like it suits you."

"You really think so?"

"Absolutely. When are you going to apply?"

"I downloaded the form last night. Can I list you as a reference? And would you look it over before I send it in?"

"Yes, to everything."

Lindsay had a determined glint in her eyes while she scanned the room. "This looks good."

"Yeah, well." I pushed curls off my forehead and took a step back. "It's getting there. I should have given the room a thorough cleaning first. I don't know why I didn't notice how bad it was when Greg and I moved the bed in here." I stomped on a dust ball as it skittered across the floor. "But first I need to run an errand. How are things downstairs?"

"Quiet. I can hold down the fort."

I cleaned up in the public restroom on the main floor. The ancient hot-water pipes clanked and vibrated but produced what I needed for a quick face- and hand-wash and hair pat-down. The radiator ticked under the frosted-glass window. It was cold out there.

What had Greg been wearing when he left? I hugged my arms across my chest and hoped he was warm enough, wherever he was. Maybe Betty would remember. That's right—he'd packed all his clothes. He could have pulled on everything—multiple layers—unless he got separated from his luggage. I leaned my forehead against the window. Where was he?

OOO

Betty met me on the front porch again. She seemed to have a sixth sense about visitors. "Come inside, honey. Have you heard anything?"

I shook my head.

"I keep thinking he would have talked to me if I'd kept my mouth shut." Betty filled the percolator from the tap.

"He told you about Angie and Lorenzo. We usually just talked about work and research, his classes. He didn't say much about his family, but I got the impression he had sisters—he certainly knew how to tease like a younger brother. But his professor only mentioned a mother."

"Oatmeal raisin?" Betty opened a Tupperware container.

"Uh, yeah. Yeah, thanks." I accepted a cookie and chewed slowly.

"He has twin sisters, a few years older. His dad left when the kids were little, and the mother sort of held things together. But I got the sense she was relieved when Greg moved out. Both of the girls married military men, and they're living overseas now. I think he's trying to figure out what a family should be like, before he starts one."

Greg was thinking about starting a family? I exhaled. Well, Greg could get a much better definition of family from Betty than he ever would from me. I bit back a smile. How like him to find the best source of information. I washed the cookie down with a slurp of hot, strong coffee.

"The reason I stopped by was to ask about the washbasin and pitcher in Greg's room. Have they been in your family long?"

"Oh my, yes." Betty adjusted the paisley scarf around her neck. "I think my grandparents received them as a wedding gift, or at least early on in their marriage. Isn't that funny? I guess like giving newlyweds a blender today. There used to be a chamber pot, too, but it's long gone. Probably broken on a trip to the outhouse."

"That's the thing. Our new display at the museum—the one Greg and I were working on this past weekend—is a collection of chamber pots."

Betty leaned back in the dinette chair and dissolved into peals of tinkly mirth until her eyes watered. I couldn't help but join in.

"That Rupert Hagg," Betty finally sighed. "What will he think of next?"

I grinned. "Well, you should see one of the chamber pots. It has exactly the same design—the blue Dutch windmills—as your washbasin and pitcher."

Betty's eyes widened. "No."

"I wondered if they originally came in matched sets, and you just confirmed it. I'm being very bold, Betty, but how would you feel about lending your washbasin and pitcher to the museum for the display?"

"I'd be delighted. It's not like I use them anymore. I just put them in Greg's room for decoration." Betty jumped up and hurried down the hall, her voice trailing after her. "I have some newspaper. I'll wrap them up for you."

I stepped off Betty's porch with two neatly masking-taped bundles in my arms, smearing newsprint all over my jacket. "I'll get you an official receipt."

"Of course, dear. There's no hurry."

"The exhibit opens tomorrow, so please come visit your treasures."

"I will, sweetie." Betty waved until I turned onto State Route 14.

Adding Betty's washbasin and pitcher meant I had to rearrange two and a half display cases, but I was able to give the matched set the entire eye-level shelf in the third case. I printed "courtesy of Mrs. Elizabeth Jenkins" cards to prop next to the two loaned pieces and also made Betty's receipt while I was thinking of it. I didn't want to risk having Betty's family heirlooms lost in the jumble should we ever dismantle the display. Cataloging had definitely improved during my tenure as curator, but there was still a huge backlog of older items needing identification numbers and descriptions. I might have to shuffle displays as more of the items in storage became available for exhibit.

I lugged the ancient resident Hoover with the frayed cloth-covered cord upstairs. The beast weighed a ton but still sucked up anything and everything without regard to race, creed, or insurance value, including floor rugs and beaded slippers if the operator wasn't careful. The exhibit of Victorian-era ball gowns had narrowly escaped an incident with the Hoover.

After banishing all dust balls and cobwebs, I smoothed the comforter on the bed and fine-tuned the furniture arrangement. I stood in the doorway and surveyed my work. The exhibit looked good, especially with the bright-yellow potty chair in the bottom corner of the last case to draw visitors' attention.

What was I going to tell the kids during the tour the next day? I usually worked up spiels in my head that covered the most interesting facts but left flexibility for answering questions. But I couldn't focus, not with worry about Greg gnawing at the back of my mind. I pulled my phone out of my pocket and dialed Sheriff Marge.

"Meredith, I'm glad you called. We got a tip. It's a long shot, but I'm organizing a search anyway. Maybe it will keep people from interrupting me."

I winced. "Where?"

"Just this side of the bluff past Milepost 134 on State Route 14. You can park off the highway there, then walk to the west of the bluff. A long-haul truck driver reported 'one of those little hybrid things, silver-colored' parked there on Sunday with the hood up. Dale's been over the site and not found any distinguishable tire marks. No sign of a car going down the embankment, but we'll have a look anyway."

"I'll be there as fast as I can, probably half an hour," I replied to dead air.

I dashed downstairs to the gift shop. "Lindsay, I'm going out. There's a search up the highway where someone might have seen Greg's car."

"I'm coming with you." Lindsay grabbed her purse and coat.

I stopped midstride.

"It's okay, isn't it? Only forty minutes until closing time, and no one's in the building right now. Visitors, I mean."

"Yeah. Let's go." I locked the big front doors behind us. "I'll drive, but I'm going to stop and pick up Tuppence. I have this probably fruitless hope her nose might be useful. And she expects the window seat, so you'll have to sit in the middle. Do you mind?"

"No problem."

OOO

Lindsay held the door open, and Tuppence jumped in while the truck was still rolling, like a touch-and-go landing. I threw it into gear and roared out of the campground. There were already half a dozen vehicles at the parking site Sheriff Marge had described. I pulled in behind Mac's step van.

I grabbed a leash from the glove box and snapped it onto Tuppence's collar. People usually drive eighty on straight stretches of State Route 14 even though the posted limit is sixty. We clung to the edge of the gravel as we walked around the bluff to a large, marshy area full of cattails and tall grass that spread for about forty acres. The cattails had exploded into what looked like giant hairballs, the kind of fluff that collects on sheep ranchers' barbed wire fences.

Deputy Dale Larson stood at the top of the embankment with a clipboard under his arm.

"Meredith, Lindsay—great. You can join the east end of the line." He pointed. Dots of brightly colored hats and jackets were scattered over the field—other searchers. But the section farthest to the right was empty.

"His car's not here. There's no way it could get far in this muck. So you're looking for small stuff—wallet, sunglasses, items of clothing, shoes, anything that might indicate Greg has been or still is in the marsh. Okay?" Dale looked at our feet. "Did you bring waders, rubber boots?"

"We didn't take the time. I'll be fine," I said.

Lindsay nodded. "Me, too."

Dale frowned and turned to the open trunk of his cruiser. He handed us each a fistful of florescent-orange nylon strips. "If you find something that looks new, within the last week or so, tie one of these to the nearest cattail. If you find anything you are certain belongs to Greg, let me know immediately—holler and wave your arms."

Dale pointed in the opposite direction. "About twenty yards this way is a pile of gravel the highway department must have left. It's the easiest way to get down to the marsh. You just sort of slide. I'll help direct you to your places in line. Once you're in the tall grass, it's hard to get your bearings."

We trotted to the gravel ramp and slid down, then jogged parallel to the embankment until we were directly below Dale. He did the tomahawk chop to line us up, and I plunged in. Within a few steps, my sneakers were soaked through, cold and gritty. Tuppence was lighter on her feet and scrabbled over the clumps of cattail roots.

"Good thing I'm not a girlie girl," Lindsay said from a couple of yards away.

I had thought that was exactly what she was—unknown facets. I stumbled and slowed, carefully scanning the ground from side to side.

Tuppence led like a pointer, stretched out in a straight line from nose to tail tip, plodding resolutely between the tall stalks. I let her pull me along and held an arm aloft to shield my face from the razor-sharp edges of the grass blades. I couldn't feel my toes anymore.

The ground rose slightly as we headed toward the tree line, and soon I was walking on firmer mud populated by fewer cattails but denser grass. I stooped to examine a cracked Bic lighter. Greg didn't smoke, but sometimes nonsmokers carried lighters for other purposes. What other purposes I couldn't quite recall. Attending rock concerts, maybe, although didn't people just flash their cell phones these days?

I didn't think it was worth a marker. Greg liked old jazz and blues, not rock. I remembered the lengthy discourse he'd given on the scratchy vinyl record sounds that were the backdrop to, in his opinion, the best Billie Holiday tracks. "They shouldn't be cleaned up too much," he'd said. "Those sounds give the feel of the smoke and scotch in her first venues—speakeasies."

I had laughed. "You were born a couple generations too late."

Tuppence veered left and pounced on a gigantic bullfrog.

"*Ooop*, leave him alone." I pulled on the leash. "He's just trying to get back to the water. Come on."

No time for dillydallying. I stepped right out of my sneaker and pitched forward onto my hands and knees, wrist-deep in the frigid muck.

"Ugh. Graceful."

Tuppence came back to see if she could help and got tangled in the leash. I pushed myself up and hopped around on the shoed foot looking for the missing sneaker.

It was vacuum-packed in mud a couple paces back. I groaned and gingerly set my stockinged foot down in the ooze. There was no other way. I had to stand on both feet to get the leverage needed.

I scooped my fingers under the heel and pried the sneaker out. It came with a long slurping sound. I didn't have anything to scrape the mud off my sock, so I jammed the extricated sneaker back on my foot. Some women paid good money for spa treatments that weren't much different. Warmer maybe, with fluffy towels and cucumber slices.

A Skoal tin, several crushed beer cans, a clear plastic Gatorade bottle half-full of yellowish liquid, a woman's red knit glove that was growing moss, and a soggy matchbook later, I looked up to see where we were. We had reached the edge of the forest. Douglas firs the size of Christmas trees grown for suburban homes stood like toddlers next to their giant parents. I spotted the top of Lindsay's hood bobbing several yards away.

I stepped a few feet to my right, turned around, and headed back toward the highway, retracing a parallel track, double-checking. An eyeball stared up at me.

"No way." I blinked.

Tuppence nosed over it, and I pulled her aside. I stooped for a better look and had the eerie feeling I was standing on the chest of a cyclops buried in the mud.

I tapped the iris with my fingernail—it was hard—and pulled the eye out. After wiping it off on my jeans, I balanced it in my palm. The eye wasn't round, or even oval—more like a simple amoeba shape. The blue-gray iris had faint striations. I shivered and rolled the eye over—no markings.

Maybe it was a theatrical prop or part of a costume. I'd never seen a glass eye in person before. But it definitely wasn't Greg's. I dropped it into my pocket.

"Okay, folks. Come on in. It'll be dark in twenty minutes," Dale yelled on a bullhorn. I trudged a beeline to the embankment and met Lindsay in the cluster of other searchers at the gravel slide.

I was grateful to see so many—Mac, Pastor Mort, several people I recognized from the Sunday potlucks, including the husband and father of the migrant-worker family.

"Thank you for helping," I said. "What's your name?"

"Jesus Hernandez. I think, what if it was one of my kids missing? So I come."

"All right, everyone," Dale announced from above. "The gravel's tricky, so we'll have to team up. Mac, can you give people a boost? Grab my hands, and I'll pull from up here. Ladies first."

Mac had his arm around my shoulders before I even knew what was happening. "Just doing what the deputy asked me to." He winked at me and then placed two firm hands on my behind and lifted.

"Woooaah," I yelped. Then Dale had a grip on my arm and hauled me up.

"You okay?"

"Yes." I tried to regain some dignity. Tuppence scrambled up the gravel slope.

Lindsay popped up right behind her. The first thing she did upon gaining her footing was brush off the seat of her jeans. "Mac is enjoying that way too much," she muttered.

The men clambered up the side in a more ungainly fashion, but one that was also less personally invasive. They preferred not to grasp hands, let alone any other body parts.

I realized I hadn't heard anyone shout for Dale's attention while they were searching. I caught up with him. "Anything?"

"Nope." He squeezed my arm. "We're not going to give up. The right tip will come in. We just have to wait."

Waiting. We were waiting to find Greg while he was waiting to be found. Pressure built in my chest. I wanted to scream, to rage against the waiting, against my own ineffectiveness. I should know where he'd gone—I should know. The pressure faded, and I went suddenly numb. I'd already racked my brain so many times. Nothing.

"Oh. I found this." I handed Dale the glass eye.

"What the—" He clicked on his flashlight and held the eye in its beam. It stared back, its surface glistening.

My stomach lurched. The thing was too real-looking.

"I wonder—" Dale murmured.

"What?"

"Probably nothing." He slipped the eye into a plastic bag and sealed it. "Thanks, though. You just never know what you'll find during searches like this."

My joints creaked as Lindsay and I strolled to the pickup, cold and bone-weary. The mud in my shoe doubled as a gel insert, cushioning and gooshing around my toes. They were my favorite sneakers, and I'd probably have to throw them away. The cell phone in my pocket rang.

"Meredith? It's Clyde. I'm checking into my hotel. I got a bit of a late start today, but I was hoping I could take you out to dinner. Greg speaks very highly of you."

I wrinkled my nose. "Uh, okay. I need some time. We've just been searching a site where Greg might have been spotted."

"Find anything?"

"No."

"When should I pick you up? I made a reservation for seven thirty at a little winery near you, the Willow Oaks. The website says they have a wood-fired oven."

I sighed. The Willow Oaks is Dennis Durante's place, and the best thing about it is the website. He hired a photographer who's great at taking shots that make things appear bigger and more glamorous than they really are. Lots of pictures of ripe grapes on vines and blue sky over the river. They forgot to show that the café is in a lean-to tacked onto a pole barn. There was certainly no need for a reservation.

Dennis is trying hard, but the town of Platts Landing just isn't trendy enough, let alone populated enough, to support a small artisan winery and wannabe farm-fresh bistro. The spot is quaint in daylight, but after dark on a cold night? I hoped Dennis wouldn't mind if I asked to sit right next to the oven, even if that meant sitting in the kitchen.

"In an hour."

"Where?"

I gave him directions to the Riverview RV Ranch.

"Spot C-17? What does that mean?"

"I live in an RV. It's the only one in the campground right now, so it'll be easy to find." I chuckled after hanging up. Clyde was in for a little culture shock.

"Greg's adviser?" Lindsay asked.

"Yeah. I guess he's trying to help."

CHAPTER 9

I dropped Lindsay off at her car in the museum parking lot, then hurried home to shower and dress. Tuppence needed a good rubbing down, too, and a large dinner and rawhide treat. I dabbed on some makeup. I tried lip gloss, but that lasted all of five seconds. I'm a compulsive lip-licker when I know there's something on them besides ChapStick. Oh, well. Clyde could either like me as is, or not—his call.

Tuppence woofed and looked at the door. There was a hesitant knock. I grabbed my coat and opened the door.

Clyde Elroy, dressed in slim dark jeans, un-tucked-in black button-up shirt, and black leather motorcycle jacket, looked the shocking antithesis of professorial. His longish hair, thinning and swept back from his forehead, could best be described as taupe. Hazel eyes, diminutive nose and chin. Middle height, probably, although I was gazing at him from the RV doorway, about eighteen inches off the ground. A hint of a paunch about his middle. The clothes and the man seemed to be at odds with one another.

He stepped forward and offered his right hand. "Meredith?"

"Hello, Clyde." I shook his hand and nearly hit him in the face because he was trying to kiss the back of my hand. Whoops. "I'm ready."

I hurried down the stairs and closed the door before Clyde could be subjected to hound inspection. No need to unnerve him so soon.

Clyde opened the passenger door of his black Cadillac sedan, and I slid in and bundled the coat on my lap. The car was warm inside.

"Interesting living arrangements," Clyde said when he was buckled in. "I take it the museum doesn't provide a housing stipend."

"Why should they?"

"Well, this far out, I thought . . ."

"I have the best river view anyone could hope for."

"Ah. The compensation of nature." Clyde's smile was papery thin. He followed the instructions of the GPS's female voice to turn left out of the campground.

"Have you spoken to Greg's mother again?"

"No. I told her I'd call when I had news. And since there's been no news, I haven't called. Unpleasant woman."

"What about his sisters? Have you talked to them?"

"Does he have sisters? I expect his mother will inform the necessary family members."

I squinted out the windshield as the headlights bore though blank darkness. "I suppose she will let Angie know, then, as well."

"Angie?"

"His girlfriend, on a dig in Turkey. I don't know her last name."

"Angie Marshall? He can't possibly be dating Angie Marshall."

"Like I said, I don't know her last name."

The GPS woman interrupted to instruct Clyde to turn off State Route 14 onto Dennis's road.

Dennis was waiting for us, long apron tied around his middle, menu cards in hand. Little beads of sweat glistened on his forehead as he led us to a small table under a propane heater hood. I pulled on my coat.

Dennis laid the menu cards in front of us and then read them out loud. "The specials today are stuffed salmon fillet on a bed of wild rice risotto with sautéed vegetables, and roast Cornish game hen on a bed of wild rice risotto with sautéed vegetables."

"Do you have any appetizers?" Clyde asked.

I quickly laid a hand on his arm. "You know, I'm exhausted from the search today. I wonder if we could skip straight to the entrée?" Not to mention that my feet were freezing on the concrete patio where the heater couldn't reach them.

Clyde grunted.

I smiled up at Dennis. "The specials sound wonderful, but I'm afraid I couldn't do them justice tonight. I know you have some great cheeses on hand. Think you could make me a grilled cheese sandwich?"

Dennis bobbed his head. "Absolutely. And you, sir?"

"I was really hoping for something from the wood-fired oven," Clyde grumbled.

"Sorry, sir. That's a summer feature."

"I'll take the game hen." Clyde tossed the menu card against Dennis's apron-clad front. "What about a wine list?"

"The new ones aren't printed—"

Clyde gave an exaggerated sigh. "A bottle of your best red—merlot."

Dennis fled to the kitchen.

"Well, we'll just have to make the best of it, then, shall we?" Clyde said.

"Of course." I gritted my teeth. "What's your research area?"

By the time my sandwich arrived, I knew, without a doubt, that Clyde, regardless of how urbane he might consider himself to be and how interesting his subject matter could have been, was also self-absorbed and fatally boring. He was a cultural anthropologist for one—himself.

Dennis rescued me. He set on the table a plate of golden, crunchy toast oozing cheese like a slow lava flow. "Muenster on sourdough.

I took the liberty of adding thinly sliced Granny Smith apple and chopped toasted walnuts. I hope it's all right."

"Dennis, you're a saint."

He ducked shyly and darted away.

"Absent-minded galoot," Clyde said. "He still hasn't brought the wine."

"I'm sure you don't mind if I dig in. So what's your next book about?"

I sent out a secret thank-you over the airwaves to Dennis for forgetting the wine. There are no taxis out here, so I needed Clyde sober enough to drive me home. Although at this point, I wouldn't have minded punching him in the chops to get his keys. Maybe he'd stop talking. I tuned him out and savored every bite.

Fortunately, Clyde was oblivious to my lack of attention. I had cleaned my plate and started to doze, then got a second wind worrying about Greg. The blue propane flames flickered and hissed overhead.

I closed my eyes and pictured a map, the route from Platts Landing to Corvallis that Greg would likely have taken. All state and interstate highways—well-traveled roads. Someone must have spotted him. I hoped that person or persons remembered seeing Greg and made the connection with the TV news segment seeking information.

The game hen arrived ten minutes after I'd finished my sandwich. Clyde forked up a mouthful of risotto, grimaced, examined his cloth napkin, reconsidered, and swallowed. I absently watched the lump move down his lengthy esophagus.

"Completely uncooked." Clyde cleared his throat.

He went at the bird with a knife and fork and sawed and sawed without gaining traction on the rubbery appendages. He sighed and set down the silverware. "Also uncooked, I'm afraid. This is inexcusable. Let's go." He laid a twenty-dollar bill on the table. "That'll cover your sandwich." He ushered me to the Cadillac.

He insisted on walking me to my door. I turned to thank him for dinner. He wasn't that much taller. I'm not sure how he got the angle, but there he was, lips mashed against mine, tongue poking around. He tasted like lettuce.

I backed up and bumped my head on the awning brace. I really wanted to spit, pull an old Amos Stanley right then and there.

"That is not—professional," I spluttered. I held up a warning finger and prepared to knee him if he came any closer. "And completely uncalled for." My heartbeat pounded in my ears.

"You're clearly distressed." Clyde retreated. "I just wanted to comfort you."

I snorted and fixed an evil-eye glare on him. Like I'd believe that.

I watched his taillights until they were safely out on State Route 14. He was the type who might sneak back around to see if I'd changed my mind. I blew out a big breath. Between Mac and Clyde, I was feeling a bit manhandled.

I brushed my teeth—twice—and gargled.

On a hunch I pulled up a professor-rating website. Eighty percent of the comments on Dr. Clyde Elroy were some variation on the "booooring—drones on and on" theme. Tell me about it.

"Don't go to class," one poster suggested. "Just attend the study sessions run by the TAs. They basically give you the test answers."

I kept skimming. A few other comments stood out:

"Got a little too friendly during office hours. I buzzed out of there and didn't go back. Aced the course anyway."

"Has his favorite graduate teaching assistants (I was not one of them) and gives them the best projects. But then they're doing his research for him, so not sure it's worth the extra attention."

"Kinda creeped me out. Kept watching me during lectures. Offered special office hours since I showed interest in the class, but I did NOT take him up on that."

The comments were all anonymous, but I had a pretty good idea of the gender of the office-hours commenters. The first of those really struck a chord. I'd had an information systems professor make a pass at me once—in the empty hallway outside his office. I'd pretended to be so naive I didn't know what he was suggesting. And then I'd skipped the rest of his classes that quarter except the final. He gave me an A.

There always seemed to be a few girls who found that kind of attention exhilarating—something about older men and the necessary clandestine nature of the affair. I figured those professors and those girls were pretty good at spotting one another.

Clyde impressed me as a coward—socially awkward but opportunistic, and apparently doing enough to keep afloat professionally. He'd written a couple of books, which universities liked to see from their professors. Maybe there was a streak of brilliance somewhere in that mind of his. Hard to tell. Greg had said Angie liked working for him.

I stretched and exhaled. No point in wasting time thinking about Clyde.

Still no sign of Greg. The end of day four. Too many days. The odds of his survival were decreasing rapidly. Greg was smart, though—practical. He'd keep his wits about him.

I fell asleep praying for Greg. God's forte is dealing with overwhelming odds, right?

CHAPTER 10

"Tell me what I can do," I begged.

"Nothing," Sheriff Marge replied.

Tuppence watched me pace from the kitchen island to the fireplace, back and forth.

"What about his cell phone? Does it have a GPS locater?"

"We tried that first thing. It didn't respond to pings, and the phone company can't triangulate it. Either the battery's dead or it's somewhere the signals can't reach."

"What kind of places?"

"Bank vaults, wells, and the bottom of rivers if the battery shorted out."

"Do you think—"

"No. I shouldn't have said that. Look, Meredith, there just haven't been any valid tips, no confirmed sightings, no CCTV video—nothing. I can't think of when we've had an adult missing person case with so little to go on. Usually the car turns up, stolen or something."

"The search yesterday? Dale said—"

"Nothing. I figured that going in, but since we had the manpower, we checked it out anyway. Clearly the car wasn't there, and we really need to find Greg's car. That would give us clues at least. It was busywork, Meredith. Sorry."

I sighed. It was hard to be angry. We were all looking for something to do, some way to feel useful—some way not to go crazy with worry. Besides, anger wasted precious gray cells. Greg hadn't left clues, so I was going to have to figure out what he'd been planning. From nothing. And fast. I just needed something—a spark, a flash of creative inspiration, a sudden psychological insight—something.

"Go to the museum. Do your job. And don't you dare hole up in your RV. You need to be around people right now. Tuppence doesn't count."

I looked at the dog stretched out on the floor. "She'd beg to differ. Anyway, I have school tours today, so you needn't worry. Take care." I hung up.

Tuppence raised her head.

"Yeah, yeah. Breakfast. I didn't forget."

I let Tuppence out, then followed and filled her bowl with kibble. I dumped out the ice-skimmed puddle in her water dish and refilled it.

Every grass blade was coated with white frost, sparkling in the weak sunlight. A wisp of fog along the riverbank was quickly burning off. Cold, but it would be beautiful today. I tipped my head back and let out puffs of breath steam like smoke signals.

If Greg was exposed, last night would have been hard to live through. He was so skinny, no built-in insulation. I hugged myself and rubbed my upper arms.

Tuppence stood on the steps and waited for me to open the door and let her back into the warm trailer.

"Right behind you, old girl."

ooo

At the museum I strolled through the quiet halls, planning the route I'd take with the kids. This would be the five-year-olds' first school visit to the museum. They would tour each year through the sixth grade. I tried to spread out what I showed each grade so the tours wouldn't be an exact repeat of the prior year.

Kindergartners were always fun—spunky, inquisitive, and easily bored. They also tended to bump into things, climb on things, and get lost in the odd nooks and crannies of the old building. Sally would perform many head counts during their visit.

I went to my office and stared out the window. A square of sunshine fell over my shoulders. I closed my eyes and concentrated on the warmth as it slowly sank in. I wanted to fall asleep and not wake up unless a happy ending was guaranteed. The pinprick nap that lasted a thousand years. I didn't need true love's kiss—I'd be satisfied with Greg's safe return.

The single buzz of an internal call interrupted my reverie.

"A school bus just pulled into the parking lot," Lindsay said.

"Be right down."

I indulged in the luxury of descending the grand staircase, then waded into the tide of little people surging through the front doors. Pink-cheeked kids in primary-colored puffy coats bounced off one another like pinballs. A few hats were already off and getting trampled on the floor. Static-y hair recently released from the hats stood on end.

I thought Fisher-Price had gotten it right when they designed the little pull-along bus with indentations for toy people inside. I'd dragged that bus everywhere as a toddler—upstairs, downstairs—and cried when I wasn't allowed to read to my friends at nap time. This was better. I grinned at my living swarm of miniature people.

A few adults ringed the periphery—chaperone parents. I waved to the graphic-designer mom I'd met at the potluck. She had the baby strapped into a carrier on her back.

Sally bustled over. "Well, here we are." She gave me a quick hug and whispered, "I'm so sorry about Greg. Mort told me you were out helping search last night. We're sure praying he'll be found—soon and safe."

I squeezed her back. "I know. Thank you."

Sally clapped her hands. "Find your partner. Line up right here in front of me." The children shuffled into a crooked line, holding hands, and looked up expectantly. "This is Ms. Morehouse, and she is the curator here at the museum. Who knows what a curator does?"

Several hands shot up. Sally pointed to a runny-nosed boy.

"You know how old stuff is and where it came from."

I grinned. "That's right. I make sure all the really neat things are on display so people can learn about them. Do you want to know what it was like to live a hundred years ago?"

While most nodded, one stubborn child in the back shook her head in an emphatic no. I ignored her.

"How about two hundred years ago?" More vigorous nodding except from the dissenter in the back.

"My grandpa is really old," another little girl offered.

"Well, we have some things that are even older than he is. Ready to go find them?" A hand waved midpack.

"Yes, Quentin," Sally said.

"I have to go to the bathroom."

"Oh dear. Maybe that should be our first stop?" She raised her eyebrows in my direction.

"Of course." I chuckled and led the way.

After all the kindergartners gained expert knowledge of the museum's restroom facilities, I walked them through the more tactile exhibits, keeping the pace up and encouraging questions. The early-appliances room was a hit, especially when the kids took turns cranking the handle on the British mangle. The rug room was appropriately vilified for its musty odor, complete with nose-pinching.

The taxidermy room with moth-eaten specimens of black bear, elk, cougar, mountain goat, beaver, opossum, golden eagle, and one sadly flaking rattlesnake generated awe and perhaps a little apprehension. Sally liked to have her class go through the exhibit because it prompted energetic discussion later, once the kids had a chance to recover.

I saved the chamber pot display for last. I stopped at the door to the bedroom and waited for the stragglers to catch up.

"This room used to be a bedroom, back when the Hagg family lived here. It was probably Bernice Hagg's room. She was the sister of the man who built the house, and she lived here for many years." She'd also died during a grand mal seizure in the kitchen, where she'd been instructing the cook how to make floating islands, but I didn't tell the kids that. "Do you remember the bathroom downstairs?"

Lots of nodding.

"This house is fancy, so it always had bathrooms. But not everyone had a bathroom in their house back then. And if they didn't have a bathroom, they would dig a big hole in the ground and put a little building over the hole for privacy and use that to go to the bathroom. Has anyone used an outhouse before?"

A sea of waving hands. I pointed at one of them.

"When we go camping, we use an outhouse," the boy said. "It's smelly and there are bugs and spiders in there."

"You don't have to flush," another kid announced.

"Yep, they're not always very nice, are they? What happens if you live in a house that doesn't have a bathroom—and it's the middle of the night . . . and it's snowing outside . . . and you have to go to the bathroom? What do you do?" I had their full attention.

"You hold it?" a girl said, her eyes wide.

"What if you can't hold it?"

"Then you wet your bed," the first boy said matter-of-factly. "Or wear a diaper."

This was met with guffaws.

"Diapers are for babies," said another voice.

"That's right." I tried to grab control. "How many of you have younger brothers or sisters who are being potty trained?"

About half of them raised their hands.

"That's so gross."

"He gets M&M's if he goes."

"Eeeww. My brother still wears diapers."

"Do any of them use a potty chair?" I shouted over the melee.

"Oh, yeah."

"One time it tipped over in the car."

"Well, guess what people used at night when they didn't have a bathroom in their house?" I asked.

They swiveled their eyes back to me, riveted.

"Potty chairs. Except they were called chamber pots. Some were big, some were small." I moved my hands with the sizes. "Some were fancy, some were plain. And everybody used them, even grown-ups. Do you want to see them?"

There was a general pushing and elbowing as they crowded into the room.

Sally caught up with me just outside the door. "This is so great," she murmured. "They're fascinated by the basics of life, especially bodily functions."

"I can't believe we paid good money to look at potty chairs," Quentin said as he craned his neck to see over the kid in front of him.

Sally whirled away, shoulders quaking. When she came back, she said in a strangled voice, "His father's the mayor. I'll have to tell him admission is free for school groups."

Giggling erupted in the bedroom.

"You're not supposed to do that," a child announced indignantly.

"I just wanted to see." The little voice ended in a whimper.

Sally frowned. "That—"

But I didn't wait for her to finish. I moved children out of the way and headed toward the two girls and one boy who were bent over the bedside chamber pot. I peered through the space between their heads to find that one of the girls was actually sitting in the chamber pot—fully clothed, but stuck.

She wriggled, her rubber-toed sneakers skidding on the floor without gaining traction. Her brown eyes filled with tears, and they dribbled down her flushed cheeks. She started shifting from side to side, rocking the chamber pot—the Dutch windmill chamber pot.

"Whoa, whoa, honey." I grabbed her under the arms and lifted her up—pot and all—and set her gently on the bed. "We'll get you out. It's okay."

The little girl's lower lip trembled.

"Paulina!" The graphic-designer mom rushed over. She glanced at me, apologetic. "She's mine."

Paulina succumbed to deep, hiccupy bawling.

I realized the room behind me was silent and turned. Twenty-three pairs of saucer eyes stared back from frightened little faces. The faster I could defuse the situation, the less traumatic for everyone.

"Everything will be all right," I announced loudly over Paulina's wails.

I leaned toward the mother. "Let's get her coat off. Too much padding."

I tugged on the coat's hem, which was wedged inside the pot's rim, while the mother pulled on the sleeves, raising Paulina's arms over her head. With a soft *phffft*, the coat came free. Paulina calmed to jerky sniffing.

"Okay, now, Paulina, I want you to lie on your side and touch your toes. Everyone can do this, right? Like Simon Says." I looked over my shoulder and caught Sally's eye. Did kids still play that game?

Sally nodded. "That's right, class. Simon says, 'Touch your toes.'"

A rustle filled the room as twenty-three children moved, most dangling their fingers in the vicinity of their toes. A couple hopped on one foot. One fell over.

Paulina slowly stretched, and I hovered. As the little body lengthened and thinned, I got a firm hold on the pot.

The mother rubbed Paulina's back. "Keep stretching, munchkin."

I felt the pot slip and eased it off.

"Simon says, 'Clap your hands three times.'" Sally beamed.

I sat on the bed beside Paulina and wrapped an arm around her. "Not too bad, was it?"

Red-rimmed eyes, like those of a sad bloodhound, turned up to me. Paulina's dark-brown hair was frizzed and half pulled out of her two side braids. She looked so woebegone that I almost chuckled. What could I say to comfort her? Instead I hugged the little girl. Paulina hugged back, wiping her nose on my shoulder.

"I'm Lauren, by the way," the mother said. "I didn't introduce myself properly on Sunday. And, uh, thank you. I'm sorry about this."

"No, I'm sorry," I said. "I want the exhibits to be hands-on, but I didn't anticipate, well—" I shook my head. "And I should have."

"No matter how prepared you are, kids will always do the one thing you didn't expect." Lauren smiled. "It's a good thing they're flexible." She took Paulina's hand, and the girl slid off the bed.

"Everyone line up," Sally called. "And what do you say to Ms. Morehouse?"

The kids chimed a syncopated "Thank you" chorus as they shuffled out of the room. Sally waved good-bye over their heads.

I turned the Dutch windmill chamber pot in my hands, scowling. This was the pot that coordinated with Betty's pitcher and washbasin. I was certain I'd placed this pot in the display to complete the grouping, and the chamber pot on the floor had been a basic enamelware model—something a child, or any visitor for that matter, could not break. It was gone.

I walked to the display case where Betty's pieces were. Another chamber pot had been moved to take the spot where the Dutch windmill pot had been. I quickly scanned the descriptions and found four pots out of place. It seemed they'd been shuffled to fill in gaps, to cover for the missing Dutch windmill pot. And that pot had replaced the enamelware one on the floor.

Just to make sure, I stepped back and counted—yes, seventy-one chamber pots, one pitcher, one washbasin, and one plastic potty chair. A chamber pot really was missing.

I knelt and peered under the bed—nothing but clean floorboards. Who would steal a chamber pot?

Frowning, I removed a child's chamber pot from a display case and set it on the floor beside the bed for the afternoon school tours. Then I returned all the other misplaced pots to their rightful places.

Downstairs Lindsay was refilling the postcard carousel.

"Did you—" I wrinkled my nose. "I know this is going to sound silly, but did you rearrange the chamber pot display?"

Lindsay frowned. "No. I never touch the displays. I'm too afraid I'll mess something up."

"Did anything look out of place to you this morning? How about the cash drawer—was the amount right?"

"Yeah." Lindsay set a stack of postcards on the counter. "What's wrong?"

"I'm trying to figure out how someone got into the building overnight and all the way up to that bedroom, rearranged the chamber pots and took one, then left without setting off the alarm."

"I think it would be kind of easy, since the motion sensors have been turned off. But who'd want to take a chamber pot?"

"Why are the motion sensors off?"

"Oh, didn't you know? I noticed when I first started working here. The motion sensors don't have red blinking lights, so I asked Rupert. He said as soon as they were installed, spiders started setting them off all the time—like several times a night. So he had the alarm company come back and disable them. He figured their presence would deter burglars, that people wouldn't know they didn't actually work."

I groaned.

I climbed the stairs to my office and phoned Sheriff Marge.

Sheriff Marge sighed. "Honestly, Meredith. With everything that's going on right now, I'm not going to worry about a missing chamber pot."

"But someone must have broken in."

"Anything else missing? Damage?"

"Not that I noticed."

"Well, until there is—" Papers shuffled in the background. "Get a new alarm system." Sheriff Marge hung up.

I frowned at Sheriff Marge's abruptness. I thought about calling her back but didn't want to antagonize her. Maybe they'd received more tips about Greg's potential location. But Sheriff Marge would have said if that was the case.

I riffled through the stacks of paper on my desk but couldn't settle down to any kind of meaningful work. It felt like everything I knew and counted on was crumbling. Greg missing was the big gaping hole. Then there were other things nibbling around the edges—Clyde's unwelcome impertinence, the absent pot, having a child get stuck in an exhibit. I clung to my chair for fear it might roll out from under me, too.

CHAPTER 11

The afternoon tour for first- and second-graders was downright dull compared to the morning tour, for which I was grateful. I led the kids through the farming implements room, the Victorian ball-gown display, and the scanty Native American artifact exhibit while Lindsay plied the patient bus driver with scorched coffee from the pot in the staff kitchen.

We watched the kids trundle back to the bus. It pulled away belching clouds of black diesel smoke.

"Do you feel a little creepy, about the chamber pots being rearranged?" Lindsay asked.

"Yeah. Would you mind taking whatever cash there is in the drawer home with you tonight?"

"No problem. Is the missing chamber pot valuable?"

"No. Probably the least valuable one of all. So whoever took it either doesn't know or doesn't care. But I'm wondering if it somehow got misplaced, if it's somewhere else in the museum."

"I hope I'm not interrupting anything, ladies. Thought I'd come see the famous Imogene."

We spun around. Clyde Elroy stood between a bookshelf and the rack of solar-system mobiles.

He looked Lindsay up and down. "I haven't had the pleasure of knowing you yet," he said, smiling in a way that looked exactly like a leer.

My blood pressure jumped so fast I thought my eyeballs might pop out. "When you said Greg couldn't possibly be dating Angie Marshall, what did you mean?" I blurted before Lindsay could be polite and introduce herself.

He looked startled. "Uh, well—it's just that Angie's a very adventurous girl."

"Obviously. She's on a dig in Turkey."

"I mean, uh, adventurous in other ways. Perhaps *experimental* is a better word. Greg, you know, seems like a traditionalist."

A series of neurons rapid-fired in my brain, and I balled my hands into fists. "You mean you had an affair with her."

Lindsay gaped, wide-eyed.

Clyde shuffled his feet. "Let's not jump to conclusions. We're adults."

"In a teacher-student relationship. That's predatory."

He blanched and let out a humorless, nervous laugh. "If anyone's predatory, it's Angie. It's well known among my peers that she makes the rounds. However, she's also very good at research."

"Get out of my museum," I said through clenched teeth. "You disgusting pissant." I lunged.

Clyde stumbled backward and retreated a little too fast for dignity. I regretted the front doors were too heavy to hit him on the backside on his way out.

I was breathing like I'd just won a hundred-meter dash.

"Wow, your vocabulary really kicks up a notch when you're mad." Lindsay was trying not to laugh. "Was that Greg's adviser?"

I grunted. I closed my eyes and focused on slowing my heartbeat. "Did I really just do that?"

Lindsay wrapped an arm around my shoulders. "Yes. I think the mama bear in you came out because you're worried sick about Greg." She shivered. "Besides, that guy deserved it. What a creep." A frown flitted across her face. "What's a pissant, anyway?"

OOO

I went to my office and Googled how long someone could live without food and water. It had rained enough lately that Greg might have a clean water supply, but he was skinny and it had been dipping below freezing at night—two strikes against his survival time. If he'd been injured, that probably counted like three or four or more strikes.

Water was the key. Without it he had three to five days. With water, but without food, he had up to three weeks, depending on his condition. It was already day five.

I needed to tackle something physical, something hard. The residual adrenaline from the encounter with Clyde still buzzed through my veins.

I went to the basement, where there's always plenty to do. Starting in the farthest, dimmest corner, I dragged furniture under a forty-watt bulb hanging from the ceiling. If the item was broken beyond repair, I kept on dragging it—over to the door leading to the exterior ramp and daylight. If it looked repairable but no longer of museum quality, I put it in another pile for Mac's review. Maybe he would want to get into the secondhand furniture business. I was pretty sure he didn't charge me enough for the display cases, so maybe the hand-me-downs could help compensate for that.

I found a rodent cage complete with spinning wheel and empty water bottle, a punching bag that weighed a ton and leaked something that was a cross between sawdust and sand, half of a Ping-Pong table, and a stack of grimy acoustic ceiling tiles. I could have been unearthing a 1960s rec room—only the wet bar and early RCA color television were missing.

A headache ballooned inside my skull. I propped open the basement door and sucked in the fresh air.

I carried a broken chair out to the container-size garbage dumpster. Plastic rustling sounds came from inside. Raccoons. Big ones. During the day?

I put a foot on the knee-high ledge that ran around the dumpster and pulled myself up. Peering over the rim, I recognized the pocketed posterior of the olive-green coveralls.

"Ford? What are you doing?"

He straightened and grinned at me. From the smell of things, he'd broken open a few bags in his rummaging. The dumpster was so large it got exchanged for an empty one only every other month, so the contents of the bags at the bottom were ripe.

"Did you lose something?"

"Lookin' for Greg. Figured this was a place you could fall into and not get back out of. 'Specially if you got knocked on the head or somethin'."

I wanted to cry. "Did you find him?"

"Nope."

"Do you need a hand getting out of there?"

"Nope." Ford grabbed the edge and launched himself up and over, landing on his feet beside me in a surprisingly agile move.

"You do that a lot?"

"Nope."

"I'm cleaning junk out of the basement. Will you help me?"

"Yep."

After a few loads had been removed from the basement and deposited in the dumpster, I asked, "How are you doing, Ford?"

"Not breakin' a sweat."

"I mean overall, in life. Are you happy?"

"Got nothin' to complain about."

"How long have you lived here?"

"My whole life."

"What's the earliest thing you remember?"

"A little orange kitten. Used to dangle string for it."

"Awww. Cute."

"Then a coyote ate it."

"Oh. Are you sure?"

"Yep."

I tried again, but Ford was talked out.

"I gotta git back to work," he said, and walked off, leaving me with a formerly turquoise Naugahyde recliner that wouldn't hold an upright position.

Fortunately, the chair was on casters. I worked the angles with sheer muscle power until I got it through the door and wheeled it up the ramp. I left it beside the dumpster, hoping that the next time the driver came to pick it up, he'd also figure out a way to take the recumbent eyesore.

I heaved the punching bag onto the recliner. It looked like a giant sausage taking a nap and could easily have been mistaken for a modern art installation. If its proximity to the dumpster had symbolic meaning, that was best left up to the viewer. I returned to the museum without looking back.

ooo

I checked the chamber pot exhibit first thing Friday morning. The basic enamelware model was back, on the floor by the bed. The child-size pot that had been on the floor was in a display case, but in the wrong spot. Again, other pots were rearranged, but in a different order from the day before.

I counted—seventy-one pots. After matching cards with pots, I discovered that the stoneware model with lid was missing. This prank was getting out of hand. How many times would it have to happen before Sheriff Marge would take it seriously? Still, I didn't want to bother her.

I left a note in the gift shop asking Lindsay to call me when she arrived. I hoped we could pin the prank on a mischievous visitor. Perhaps the same person had visited both Wednesday and the day before—Lindsay would remember. But if it wasn't a repeat visitor, then someone was breaking in.

It was a distraction I didn't need. Day six. I chafed in frustration. Why couldn't I find a clue, even a tiny one—something to get me started on Greg's trail?

The hours passed in mind-numbing monotony. Lindsay confirmed there had been no repeat visitors in the past few days, not even people whom she was aware knew one another who might pass on the prank responsibility, relay baton–style.

By closing time I'd formulated a plan to catch the perpetrator. Not as good as finding Greg, but it was something. And I could do it without bothering Sheriff Marge. The high school football team was at an away game, so it wasn't like I had anything else to do except sit in my recliner and talk to a dog.

I went home for a quick grilled cheese sandwich, which paled in comparison to Dennis's masterpiece, and changed into my darkest warm clothes. The museum's thermostat was set to a chilly fifty-eight degrees during off-hours. I filled a thermos with coffee, apologized to Tuppence for leaving her behind, and drove back to the museum.

Anyone familiar with the museum would know I was inside if they saw my truck parked nearby, so I nosed into a spot along the riverbank next to the marina's boardwalk.

The Burger Basket & Bait Shop floated empty and forlorn. Rusty padlocked chains looped through the handles on the outdoor bait coolers. A few covered sailboats and cruisers bobbed in their slips, but most recreational boaters had towed their craft to winter storage.

A tug droned on the water, pushing four loaded barges. In the last yellow sunset glow that channeled up the gorge between cobalt hills, I squinted and made out the word *Tidewater*—a familiar tug-and-barge line along the Columbia and a luxury model, as tugboats went, bristling with antennas. Perfect white with dark-green stripes that looked black in the dusk. Nary a spot of rust. Definitely not Pete's clunker.

I admired Pete for having the guts to work as an independent contractor and make the powerful transport companies share the lanes. Slow and steady. Steady and slow. He sure was taking his time about asking me out.

Or maybe he had absolutely no interest, and here I was hyperventilating at the faintest hint of attention. At my age my hormones ought to be dormant, if not flat-out deceased. Phooey.

Waiting for full dark, I watched the tug's lights dwindle downriver until its rolling wake came in and slapped against the rocky shore. The floating dock emitted syncopated metal-on-wood screeches and mortal groans as the swells traveled beneath. Moored boats thudded against their old tire bumpers.

I hiked up the rise, through leaf drifts in the county park, and skirted around the museum to the basement door, noticing for the first time the scanty exterior lighting.

Spotlights hidden in the landscaping pointed up at the edifice, giving it an eerie flashlight-under-chin appearance, but very little light was directed at the base of the building.

I let myself in, turned the alarm off since it didn't do much good anyway, and locked the door behind me. I felt my way upstairs and entered the chamber pot exhibit bedroom. One of the exterior spotlights shone on the uncovered window, flooding the room with a cool halogen approximation of moonlight. The chamber pots were as I'd left them—all in the correct order.

I tested the hinges on the door to the adjoining bathroom. They squealed like a rusty swing set. To discourage visitors from poking around, the door was normally kept closed, but not locked, since it locked from the inside.

The water had been turned off in the mansion's fourteen unused private baths to reduce maintenance costs. Most fixtures were original and therefore leaky. We couldn't afford to open the museum on a Tuesday morning and find that an upstairs bath had been flooding the rooms below for a couple of days.

I eased into the bathroom and left the door open a couple inches. I settled into a cross-legged position in the claw-footed tub—the chamber pot on the floor by the bed directly in my line of vision—and leaned against the cold enameled cast iron.

Fifteen minutes later my legs were asleep. Darts jabbed into my calves, quads, hamstrings, and buttocks when I stood. I had to give them a few minutes before I was able to lift one leg and then the other over the side of the tub. Even then it felt like I was stepping on a bed of nails.

I clenched my teeth, pulled the door open to the accompaniment of a grating yowl, and added WD-40 to my mental shopping list. I grabbed a pillow off the bed and plumped the other one to hide its absence.

Leaving the bathroom door open a few more inches this time, I plopped the pillow in the tub. This stakeout business was getting old in a hurry. Stretching out as far as possible, I rested the base of my skull on the tub's rolled edge.

Ah, this was more like it. The RV had only a tight squeeze of a shower stall. There wasn't room for a full-size tub. I hadn't had a bubble bath of rose petals, milk, and honey in years. Not that I'd ever been a tub person, but soaking was a luxury that became more desirable simply because it was out of reach.

I might have dozed off.

My eyes flew open—a hulking form stood next to the bed. A soft rustling of rubbing fabric, then the distinctive *zzzipp* of a metal zipper.

He was going to steal several pots this time. Probably had a big zippered duffel bag to load them into. I sure wasn't going to let that happen.

I hadn't really thought this far along in my plan, but surprise was on my side, right? Heart pounding, I rose fluidly and leaped.

My foot snagged on the tub's high edge, and the full weight of my hurtling body slammed against the bathroom door. I caught the glass doorknob under my chin on the way down and went out cold.

OOO

Someone pinched my nose. Hard. I flapped my arms at the perpetrator, but they didn't move like they were supposed to—they were sucked under by a blurry sea of black-and-white one-inch hexagon tiles. I was floating—swimming—swirling. My head felt like it was trapped in a trash compactor. Blazing light stabbed through my eyelash filter. I groaned.

"Wake up." Someone jiggled me.

"Uhhhooooh," I said, louder. A huge head blocked the glaring overhead light.

I opened my eyes in the shadow. "Ford," I croaked.

"Yep." He grinned, just inches away. His breath smelled as though he'd had sauerkraut for dinner, and I thought pinching my nose was now a good idea. "Can you get up?"

"I jesht want . . . lie here frwhile."

He sat back and the light stung my eyes again.

"'Kay. Gemme up."

He slid me around and propped me against the wall.

"Oooooh." I slumped forward and dropped my head in my hands. A wave of nausea surged through my stomach and then returned to slosh the detritus around. "Shick."

Ford jumped over me, through the doorway, and dashed back to slide a chamber pot in front of me—almost in time. How could grilled cheese get so putrid in just a couple hours? Ford grabbed the roll of toilet paper off the holder and swabbed the chunky, yellowish-mauve puddle on the floor.

If the water was turned off, why was there still toilet paper in here? At least reason was returning. I looked at Ford. His coveralls were unzipped to the waist, revealing grungy red long underwear underneath. I didn't need to see the flap in the back to know it was a union suit.

"Why're you here?" I asked.

"Borrowin' a pot. Were you tryin' to scare me, hidin' in here? I almost shit my pants."

"It's you. Why?"

"Why what?"

"Why aren't you using your bathroom?"

"Somethin's wrong with the plumbin'. Backed up."

"You should have told me. Sooner."

"That pot"—Ford jerked his head toward the bedroom—"is like one we had when I was a little 'un. Reminded me."

I rested my head against the wall and closed my eyes. I should have checked on him at the first indication things weren't right—that night in the pickup when his clothing stank. I should have known. Ford was always saying he had nothing to complain about, even if he really did.

"Take the pot home with you until we can get your plumbing fixed. I'm sorry, Ford."

"Thanks, Missus Morehouse."

I needed to grill him about how he'd gotten into the locked museum, but later. "Thanks for helping me."

"Yep. See you later."

I kept my eyes closed and listened to his departure. There was a scrape on the wood floor as he scooped up the chamber pot, then he clumped down the hall. I lost his footsteps after the stairs. No clue about how he'd entered.

I probed my jaw with my fingers and found a painful lump in the squishy part under my chin. It was so swollen it pushed my tongue against the roof of my mouth.

I didn't taste blood, though. Of course, I'd just barfed. It hurt to swallow. There had to be more damage, and I moved my hand over the rest of my head. A goose egg on the upper right quadrant. My neck felt sprained.

My right hip ached and my right knee throbbed. I pulled up my pant leg and found the entire kneecap already purple and puffy. Jumping out of bathtubs was for younger people. Not my brightest moment.

Sitting on a cold, hard floor wasn't going to help. I needed ice packs in strategic spots and a soft bed. My brain must have taken a knocking.

I gulped air and focused on the one spot in the room that wasn't moving—my left foot. Everything else was going around like a salad spinner.

I used the doorknob to leverage myself to a standing position. The door swayed on creaking hinges but held me upright.

I shuffled out of the room, down the hall to the stairs, and across the long ballroom. It felt like days, the minutes measured in steps. Slowly. Slowly. Slowly. The keys were in my jeans pocket, where they were supposed to be. The night air was so cold it froze the boogers in my nose until they crinkled. But it felt good. Haze lifted from my addled brain.

I strode steadily, arms out for balance like a tightrope walker, and kept up the pace all the way across the park and down the slope to my truck. I opened the door, slid in, stuck the key in the ignition, and flipped on the headlights.

Out of habit, my hand kept moving to the seat belt while my mind tried to make sense of the scene illuminated in the high beams. At the end of the floating boardwalk, two men—no, three—were locked in a forceful embrace. The guy in the middle was not happy about it. His arms flailed. Long arms. He was a head taller than the others. Greg was tall like that.

The man behind the sandwiched guy looked my way, and his mouth opened. He shouted, but I couldn't make out the words. He had something in his hand, something with a bright-yellow handle—he whacked it against the middle guy's head. The tall man slumped, and the front man let him fall to the dock.

CHAPTER 12

I shot out of the truck and flew across the gravel and down the slippery ramp to the boardwalk. The man who'd been the rear guard in the tussle—who also seemed to be in charge—leaped into a boat and fired up the outboard motor. He motioned to the second man, and together they tried to shove the inert tall man into the boat.

I was close enough to hear the splash just as the boat drifted away from the dock, and the body missed the bow. The men stopped, stunned, and stared at the inky water lapping against the bumpers.

My pounding tread reverberated in my ears and must have in theirs, too, because their heads jerked toward me. Then the second man jumped into the boat, and they roared away into the black night—no lights, just rapidly fading engine noise.

I skidded to a stop and dropped at the edge of the dock where the tall man had gone into the water, yelping when my right knee hit the rough planks. Nothing. My flashlight was back in the museum, and the truck's headlights shone straight off the edge of the dock, leaving everything black below.

I plunged my arm into the icy water, reaching for hair, clothing—anything. He was so close—so close. Why hadn't he called out to me? Had he seen me? My arm went numb and my fingers cramped. I might have been bashing them against a support post for all I knew.

Tears filled my eyes and I squeezed them out. I fished the phone out of my pocket and dialed Sheriff Marge with shaky fingers.

I knew I didn't make sense but said the words *marina* and *Greg* enough times that I was sure Sheriff Marge would come. Then I pulled my knees to my chin, shivering. I tried to think but couldn't get very far, my thoughts elbowing one another out of the way. Why had Greg been here? Where had he been until now? How long would he last in the frigid river? I was blubbering.

Dale arrived first. He swaddled me in a blanket and practically carried me to his squad car. Sheriff Marge rocketed into the parking lot, light bar swirling red and blue. She launched out of her Explorer like a boulder out of a slingshot.

"She's a mess," Dale said, "but what I can gather is that Greg was held by two men. One hit him on the head, so he was unconscious when he was dumped in the water. The two men took off in a motorboat downriver."

"I called search and rescue and the fire department. We'll get divers in the water. Let me talk to her." Sheriff Marge motioned Dale back to the scene and took his place holding me up.

"I should have gone in." I said. "I could have saved him."

"Don't be stupid," Sheriff Marge said. "Current's too strong, even here at the edge. And the water temp—" She shook her head. "Dive crews will pick him up."

"Dead. Drowned."

Sheriff Marge didn't answer. She enveloped me in an enormous bear hug. Then she pulled away. "You smell like puke." She grabbed my chin in her pudgy hand and looked in my eyes. I winced and let out a whimper of pain. "Have you been drinking?"

"No. Slipped in the tub in the museum and probably gave myself a concussion."

"What were you doing in a bathtub in the museum at two a.m.?"

"Staking out the phantom rearranger. It's Ford, and no big deal. He won't do it again."

Sheriff Marge stared at me so oddly that I wondered if what I was saying in my mind and what was coming out of my mouth were two different things. I managed a weak smile and tried to appear credible. "Really. Mystery solved."

Sheriff Marge's eyes narrowed. "Tell me what you saw."

"Not much because he was in shadow, and then I face-slammed the doorknob. But Ford admitted it. He has childhood memories of—"

"Meredith!"

"What?"

"Tell me what happened at the end of the dock."

Right. The important thing. I tried to collect the shattered scenes of the past few minutes. I started from when I turned on the truck's headlights.

"Are you sure it was Greg?" Sheriff Marge interrupted.

"He was tall like Greg, but I couldn't see his face—just from the side."

"What was he wearing?"

"Uh, jeans and jacket—tan. Greg wears a tan windbreaker."

"Was he wearing glasses?"

"I don't think so. But the way he was struggling with those men, they could have come off."

"Okay. Now tell me about the other men."

"Shorter. Dark hair. The one who looked my way had a mustache." I scowled.

"What?" Sheriff Marge prompted.

"They weren't from around here."

"Meaning you didn't recognize them?"

"No—I mean yes. But they weren't wearing the right clothes. Too citified. Shoes that slipped on the wet dock. That's why they were having trouble forcing Greg into the boat. Slacks, not jeans or Carhartts. Hair slicked back—gelled or something. Nobody around here looks like that, even the people I don't know."

Sheriff Marge chuckled. "That's called profiling."

"It works, doesn't it?"

"Yes. Criminals share common characteristics. Hair gel being one of them."

"I'm serious. Like what you said about knowing people. I know this."

"Okay. What about the boat?"

"I didn't see it well, either. Normal aluminum fishing boat with an outboard motor that fired on the first try. Not fancy. Bench seats."

"I'll get the marina manager down here. See if anyone's boat's missing." Sheriff Marge stepped to the open door of her Explorer and called Nadine, the sheriff's department dispatcher and office manager.

The volunteer fire department's small convoy coasted into the parking lot, lights flashing but no sirens. Sheriff Marge trotted over to the captain and instructed him to aim their spotlights at the end of the dock. Then a steady stream of people arrived and stood around, watching the black river slither by.

Dale cordoned off the crime scene, but there was no evidence to retrieve. No cigarette butts, gum wrappers, smashed eyeglasses, or blood. The marina manager confirmed all year-rounders were in their slots, so the bad guys had brought their own transportation. Which explained why the motor had started on the first try.

A helicopter whop-whopped overhead and flashed a spotlight over the marina. The beam settled on Sheriff Marge as she waved her arms, then pointed to her ear. She keyed her radio to Nadine. "I need to talk to Henry. What channel is he on?" She heard something in the static and poked buttons until she found the right frequency. "Henry. Marge. Do you copy?"

"Loud and clear."

"White male, midtwenties, six and a half feet tall, tan jacket and jeans, went in the river off the end of this dock about half an hour ago. Unconscious. So track along the north bank for three miles down, then come on back. Okay?"

"Gotcha." The helicopter spun, tail up, and buzzed slowly downriver.

"And if you see an aluminum fourteen-footer with two guys in it, let me know."

"Okey-dokey."

"Who is that?" I asked.

"Henry Parker. Retired army chopper mechanic. Builds his own experimental aircraft now. I worry someday I'm going to have to pick up his pieces spread across several square miles. But he has the keenest eyesight of anybody I've ever met." Sheriff Marge patted my shoulder. "He's the best bet we have. He'll at least pinpoint locations where the dive team should start."

"You don't think Greg sank straight down when he was rolled off the dock?"

"We'll check everything as soon as the dive team gets here, but his body would have been buoyant. He would move with the current until snagging on something. That doesn't mean he'll be on the surface, though." She grabbed my elbow and looked steadily into my eyes. "His prospects are grim, Meredith. You know that."

I swallowed and nodded.

The radio crackled. "Dale here. I have a few boat owners on site now. We're sending out three search parties. One close in. One starting a mile down, the other two miles down."

"Okay," Sheriff Marge replied. "Since it'll be another hour before the dive team gets here, I'm taking Meredith to the office. I'll be in contact."

I opened my mouth, but Sheriff Marge growled, "Don't argue. Nadine will keep an eye on you. You're still loopy. And you'll be able to hear everything that's going on. Get in."

The sheriff's office was in a small modular building set on concrete blocks in the cracked asphalt parking lot of an abandoned grocery store. The jail was in the dank basement of the county courthouse, but they'd run out of office space down there years ago. Taxpayer money sprang for the decrepit store building and land in the hope that someday property values would go up and the resulting revenues would cover a remodel to make a state-of-the-art correctional facility. Until then the sheriff and her deputies camped out in the parking lot.

The steps creaked in warning as Sheriff Marge lumbered up them and swung open the steel door. "Nadine," she barked, "Meredith's my only witness to the kidnapping/potential drowning incident, and she has a concussion. She's not to leave until I get back. You can bench her or you can put her to work."

Nadine was in the full regalia of the late fifties, which was probably when she'd graduated from high school—thinning platinum-blonde hair teased into a sparse bouffant, chocolate-brown symmetrical arches drawn about an inch higher than where natural eyebrows should have been, fluttery fake eyelashes, sticky princess-pink lip gloss, and foundation used as mortar to smooth over wrinkles.

She wore a white turtleneck, and her breasts jutted to prominent points—an architectural marvel. Her blue-veined, knobby-knuckled hands showed her age, but chunky rhinestone rings on several fingers complemented pearlescent acrylic nails. "Have a seat," she said in a throaty smoker's voice.

"I have to make some calls," Sheriff Marge said, heading down the short hall.

I perched on the front edge of the only visitor seating available, a ratty lime-green couch that looked as though it had been left over from someone's garage sale—even when offered for free there had been no takers.

Nadine rose to refill her coffee mug, revealing a pair of tight red pants underlined by an amazing amount of girdling. She had the silhouette of a twenty-year-old, balanced on three-inch gold satin peep-toe pumps. Matching toenail polish made an appearance in the openings.

I realized I was staring. And that my headache had returned with dull, throbbing insistence.

"So you saw it, huh?" Nadine asked.

I nodded.

"Well, I seen plenty in my time." A whoosh of air escaped from Nadine's padded chair as she sat down. "Coffee's free if you want any." She waved toward the open box of red stir-sticks and sugar packets on the creamer-gritted counter. Self-service.

Sheriff Marge stormed back. "I'm going to the marina. I'll let you know if anything comes up. Nadine, thanks for coming in."

My jaw dropped. Nadine had come in for this—looking like that? She must sleep fully made up and completely corseted.

The floor quaked as the steel door banged shut and Sheriff Marge rumbled down the stairs.

"Have you worked here long?" I ventured.

"Since 1962, when I married a deputy and offered to help type his reports." Nadine sipped from the lipstick-rimmed mug. "Should have known better."

"Than to start typing reports?"

"Than to marry a cop."

"Oh." I frowned. "So you divorced him?"

"Didn't get a chance. Widowed. Three times now." Nadine sighed like it was all their fault.

"I'm sorry."

Nadine emitted a harsh laugh that turned into a coughing fit. "That's all right. I'm working on number four."

"Really? Anyone I know?"

Nadine looked around like we weren't the only two people in the building, then leaned forward, her breasts shoving papers out of the way on her desk. "Julian Joseph."

Another Joseph. I had only heard of them, the elusive wealthiest family in the county. I did some quick math. If there was a son a little older than Lindsay, then his father must be at least a decade, and up to two decades, younger than Nadine. Maybe Nadine's intended was an uncle or grandfather. How many Josephs were there?

The diversion of Nadine's potential love life didn't alleviate the overwhelming numbness cloaking my brain. But I didn't want to think about reality. Not yet. "Well, good luck," I said.

Nadine rattled on about her hopes for the future, and the sound of her voice became mushy white noise. I slowly tipped over and sank into cushions that formed taco shells around my body.

CHAPTER 13

I woke up at eye level with corn-chip crumbs embedded in the rough weave of the lime-green cushions. Someone was jiggling my foot. Gray daylight seeped through the dusty aluminum-framed windows. And then I remembered.

"Did you find him?" I asked, pushing myself upright.

"Not yet," Sheriff Marge said.

A tall, muscular man stood next to her. He wore a felt Stetson, inside. It was probably glued to his head. He also wore a hefty canvas field jacket and creased jeans over scuffed cordovan cowboy boots. He had odd golden eyes that gazed intently, rarely blinking—like an eagle's. And permanently tanned, lined skin. An all-weather sort of man. The boots weren't for show.

"This is Julian Joseph." Sheriff Marge gave a stiff nod in his direction.

"Nice to meet you." I darted a quick look at Nadine's desk, but it was unoccupied. Missing the chance of a lifetime.

"Seems we may have the same problem," Julian said in a drawling baritone.

I looked from him to Sheriff Marge. Obviously I'd missed something while I'd been sleeping.

"Julian's son, Bard, may or may not have also been missing for a few days," Sheriff Marge said.

"Why?" I asked. Stupid question.

"It's possible he has more of a reason to go missing than Greg," Sheriff Marge said. She held up a picture. "Is this the man you saw, who was knocked unconscious?"

I took the head shot. It looked like a high school yearbook photo. A young man with dark hair and eyes trying to appear strong and manly by not smiling at the camera. His little scowl came across as a pout.

"That picture's six years old, but it's the best one I have," Julian said. His eyes bore into mine, and they weren't hopeful.

"Is he your height?"

"A couple inches taller."

Tall, from a distance, with dark hair like Greg's. The assailant who'd turned to look at me—that face I'd never forget. But the man in the middle? "It all happened so fast. I just assumed it was Greg." I squeezed my eyes shut and sighed. "I can't be sure." I handed the photo back.

High heels clumped on the steps outside. Julian reached over and opened the door for Nadine, who carried a paper grocery sack. She performed a slow, slinky catwalk all the way to her desk. Julian seemed oblivious to her protruding breasts and swiveling hips.

"I got y'all some breakfast." Nadine even put on a drawl for him.

She unloaded toaster strudel, toaster waffles, and microwaveable sausage sandwiches, all in boxes. I recognized them from the freezer section of Junction General, the fastest food in town. Nadine plunked kiddie squeeze boxes of apple juice beside the entrées.

"Can I get something started for you?" She batted her fake eyelashes at Julian.

"No, thanks. I'll stick with coffee."

Sheriff Marge tore open the strudel box. "Grab what you need, Meredith. Henry located two spots he thinks the dive team should check. You can come if you stay out of the way. They've cleared the area around the marina. No body."

I stood. "Okay, thanks. Bathroom?"

Sheriff Marge waved a strawberry pastry toward the hallway. I locked myself in the Spartan room and didn't recognize the freakish specter in the mirror. My hair was plastered to the side of my head—the side I'd slept on—and the imprint of couch upholstery was still deeply embedded in my cheek. A trail of dried drool crazed the skin at the corner of my mouth. I looked closer. My chin was a ghastly shade of aubergine and still very sore. Good thing I wasn't trying to pull one over on the richest guy around. I flushed and washed and fluffed and rejoined the others.

Sheriff Marge handed me the open strudel box and an apple juice. "They'll thaw out on the way," she said. "Julian, it's your call."

"I'll meet you there," he said.

I felt like I kept missing the important stuff. "Julian just reported his son missing now?" I asked once Sheriff Marge picked up speed on the highway.

"He's a private person. Always has been."

"So private you can't tell me what's going on?"

Sheriff Marge looked at me over the tops of her glasses. "All right. Julian's wife died about fifteen years ago. Good woman. He didn't handle his grief in the best way for the boy or himself. Bard rebelled, mostly in passive ways, trying to get his dad's attention. Didn't work. Then he went off to college in California, dropped out, scrounged around, and, I think, ended up couriering drugs for a cartel—probably Sinaloa."

Sheriff Marge shifted to her left and hitched up her gun belt to move her pistol out from under her bulging hip. "He's only had intermittent contact with Julian for the past few years. Then he showed up, about a week ago, said he wanted to settle down, live at home for a while. Naturally Julian was pleased but also wise enough to know Bard had ulterior motives." She looked over at me again. "Okay. This is the confidential part, for now."

I nodded.

"The marijuana grow we found a couple weeks back—it was on Julian's property. Julian has so much property I'm sure there's a lot going on he doesn't know about. The grow was well hidden. So well hidden that we think someone who was familiar with the land planned it."

"Bard."

"Possibly. And then we raided it. Which could get him in a lot of trouble with people who don't accept excuses or apologies."

"Wow."

"I haven't made any public statements about the seizure because I wanted to see how things would shake out—see if we could find some of the workers. A grow that size meant several people were tending the place, plus they had to have a boss keeping tabs on them. It's worth over forty million dollars."

"Wow."

"Yeah. I talked things over with Julian, and he was keeping an eye on Bard, which was easy because he was hanging around the ranch, mostly. But on Thursday Bard told the housekeeper, Esperanza, he was going for a drive, and he didn't come back. He's done that before—tends to leave without explanation. Telling Esperanza was a new level of accountability for him. But now we think he might not have left of his own accord."

"Is Bard an only child?"

"Yeah."

"Wow," I whispered one more time.

Sheriff Marge slowed and pulled off the highway into a gravel turnout. Then she followed muddy tire tracks that wound between the massive trunks of old-growth fir trees. Underbrush scraped the sides of the Explorer as Sheriff Marge alternately gunned and eased the accelerator to fight through axle-crunching potholes. We emerged in a meadow clearing where the grass had been shorn to the nubs by deer.

The clearing was full of pickups and cars marked with various search and rescue organizations' logos. A van's rear doors were wide open, forming a command center. A couple of wet suits were flopped over the doors. The few people standing around wore orange vests and radios clipped to their belts. Extra oxygen tanks lay in a neat row on the ground nearby.

"We have to go on foot the rest of the way," Sheriff Marge said. "This is the closest rendezvous spot."

Julian pulled up next to us in a brand-new bronze-colored Ford F-450, the powerful diesel engine making a huge racket. He shut it down, jumped to the ground, and opened my door.

"Ever watched a dive team work?" he asked.

"No."

"Me neither."

Sheriff Marge waved to the men by the van, then headed toward a trail of trampled ferns that disappeared into the trees. I picked up the rhythmic rushing sound of the river after a hundred yards. There was no bank—just a steep drop-off.

A cluster of men stood near the edge. The burliest one was feeding a yellow nylon rope into the river. I stretched to see, and a few minutes later, a diver in scuba mask and hood popped up beside where the rope went into the water. He went back down just as quickly.

The dive team's boat was anchored twenty yards offshore. A second diver tipped over the side of the boat and disappeared in the water.

An uprooted tree, long denuded but still with an intricate pattern of crisscrossing branches at one end and crisscrossing roots at the other end, was wedged perpendicular to the cliff face, probably pressed against boulders below the surface by the current's force. Flotsam was trapped in the branches—fishing line glistening like cobwebs, the carcass of a Canada goose, chunks of lumber, an empty plastic two-liter bottle.

The yellow rope inched toward the tree, and I guessed it was tied to the first diver.

I stared at the muddy water gurgling around the tree until my eyes burned. I willed something to surface, some sign of Greg or Bard. Then I realized that if the dive team found anything, it would be a confirmation of death.

I prayed with greater vehemence that the divers would have to give up empty-handed. Better to keep hope than have it crushed. For how long, though? I glanced at Julian. He was focused on the point where the yellow rope entered the water—just as I had been. First his wife, now his son.

Maybe watching wasn't such a good idea. I didn't want his last memory of his son to be whatever the divers brought up. I touched his shoulder.

"I'd like to go back. I'm not sure I can handle this." I gestured toward the river. "I know Sheriff Marge needs to stay. How would you feel about driving me to the museum? I understand if you want to be here."

Julian shook his head. "Glad to." He took my elbow and led me back to his truck.

We made the journey in silence. The throb of the diesel engine lulled me into a semi-trance as I nestled in the cushy leather bucket seat. I thought about staying there—right there—cocooned, until the horribleness was over. Julian could drive forever—to someplace where there weren't rivers people drowned in.

Julian pulled into the museum parking lot and turned off the engine.

"I'm sorry," I blurted. "I'm so sorry. If I had gotten there a little sooner, if I had dived in right away, things might be different. Whether it's Greg or Bard, I let him go." I stretched the fingers of both hands, then clenched them into tight fists as if reenacting what could have been. "I let him go."

Julian glared in a way that froze the words in my mouth. "The stupid thing about these trucks is the center console," he said.

He opened his door and jumped out, hurried around the front of the truck and wrenched open my door. He half lifted, half slid me out and pulled me hard into his chest.

"It is not yours to bear. Do you understand? It is not yours to bear," he said in a fierce whisper. "It's mine. I drove Bard away. I made him come to this. And if it's Greg"—he tipped my head up to look in my face—"you're more to him than his own family. Sheriff Marge told me."

"Not enough to give my life for him. I thought about that, you know, at the edge of the dock."

He eased his grip but kept his arms around me. "Guilt by omission is agony compared to guilt by commission. It has no boundaries—no edges. It poisons your soul." He shifted his gaze to the river. "Meredith, don't let your mind go there. God knows we are but dust, and He is gracious accordingly."

I wasn't even sure I knew what that meant, but I nodded dumbly.

"Are there people in there for you?" he asked, tipping the Stetson toward the museum.

I nodded.

The muscles in his lower jaw worked, and he released me. At the front doors, I looked over my shoulder. Nothing seemed real anymore. Julian was standing by his truck, watching back with those golden eyes.

CHAPTER 14

Lindsay, on the other hand, was very real, and very sick. Her nose was red and raw around the edges, her eyes bloodshot and watery.

"Hey," she said when I came in, then coughed—a dry, hacking fit that left her wheezing. "I heard," she gasped. "They find anything?" She blew her nose in a shredded Kleenex.

"No. Good grief, Lindsay. You shouldn't be here."

"It's not like there's anybody else." Lindsay managed a wobbly smile. "And we've had tons of visitors already."

I checked the clock—just before noon. It was Saturday. "Can you hang on for another half hour? I need to change and feed Tuppence, then I'll come back and fill in for you. You should be in bed, or at least on the couch watching daytime television."

"Cooking shows," Lindsay rasped. "That's what my mom watches during the day." Her eyes welled up. "I'm sorry, Meredith. It must have been awful for you."

I nodded. "I need to think about something else for a while. Minding the gift shop will be perfect. I'll hurry."

I jogged to my truck, which sat alone in the marina parking lot, my right knee reminding me of the pounding it had taken last night. Yellow crime scene tape still marked off the last twenty feet of the dock. It twisted and flapped in the omnipresent breeze that rippled down the gorge.

I sped home, safe in the knowledge that all available law enforcement personnel were involved in the search effort.

Tuppence was overjoyed to see me and to eat—mainly to eat, but she did leave her food bowl twice to check on what I was doing in the bedroom. I showered quickly, brushed my teeth, and put on presentable, museum-worthy clothes. I left a rawhide chew toy with the neglected hound as consolation.

I shooed Lindsay away after getting the scoop on how many visitors were currently traipsing about the museum. Standard procedure is to count how many enter and how many leave to make sure no one is locked in the building overnight.

A family with three adolescent children came into the shop to browse, and I helped the youngest sift through a container of polished river rocks for just the right one to take home as a paperweight. The image of Greg's body skimming with the current over a bed of river rocks flashed into my mind, and I had to walk quickly away—stare out the window for a while. It was a relief when the family finally left.

The museum settled into its usual popping-and-creaking silence. The building seemed to exhale every time a blast of warm furnace air whooshed through the ductwork. Moldings dried and shrank a little more, widening cracks. Plaster chinked and sifted white powder down as dust. Windows whistled softly as drafts fingered their way in.

Early in my tenure, I had decided the mansion is a girl, the same way ships are always referred to as *she*. I felt an affinity for the old spinster. We both needed space to rest.

I added to the exit tally as an older couple waved on their way out. I sat on the bar stool behind the counter and twined my feet around the rungs.

I thought about Julian. He'd been so intense—probably his normal mode. It was the eyes. Why had he said I meant more to Greg than his own family? Did I? Surely his mother . . . and yet where was his mother?

Clyde was my only avenue for contacting Greg's family. I should probably call him. I hoped I'd startled him enough to make him reform. Maybe now he'd think twice before bedding the next enticing female student to come his way.

No, I wasn't ready to talk to Clyde. I'd wait to call until I had real news, encouraging news.

A hunched man wearing a long trench coat entered the gift shop and started browsing the perimeter. People always do that—work from the outside in. I didn't pay much attention except to register, vaguely, that his head was too big for his body. The disproportion was exaggerated by a large John Deere baseball cap.

My stomach growled. I'd forgotten to grab any food on the short layover at home. I wondered if Gloria had any Granny Smith apples and Muenster at Junction General. She always has cheese and apples, but special varieties are hit-and-miss. Maybe I could re-create Dennis's glorious sandwich. I shook my head. How could I think about food when the dive team was scouring the river for a body—maybe Greg's body?

"Pusht tha monr iner." A gnarly hand shoved a stained pillowcase across the counter. Pungent menthol or eucalyptus aftershave odor floated with it.

"Huh?" I wrinkled my nose and looked up, into the deep twin holes of a double-barreled shotgun. My mouth fell open.

The John Deere man repeated the instruction, which I gathered to mean I should put valuable things inside the pillowcase. At first I thought he had a speech impediment, but no, his teeth slid around while he talked. It was some kind of denture fixture that he kept trying to suck back in while he was speaking. It crossed my mind that he'd stolen the teeth, too, since they obviously weren't made to fit him. He seemed too young to need false teeth.

It's weird, the things that pop into your head when someone's pointing a shotgun at you. Like the fact that I didn't know any men who wore aftershave, at least not the potent kind that creates an aura with a five-foot radius. My eyes watered. The stuff singed my nose hairs. I didn't want to touch the pillowcase. It was filthy.

I opened the cash drawer. There was hardly anything in it, and the bills were so light he would think I was handing back an empty bag. I needed something heavy—quick.

The man swiveled his neck around, nervous. I opened the drawer below the cash register and tossed a tape dispenser in the pillowcase—the weighted kind with sand in the base. That should help. I grabbed a handful of the ladies' name magnets and dropped them in. They clattered against the tape dispenser.

The man swerved the gun back to aim at my chest. "Hurst ppt." He wiped his mouth on his sleeve.

I pulled my hand up to the cash drawer, where he could see it, and grabbed the pennies first. They jangled into the pillowcase.

"Bllsp."

I removed the stack of ones from their slot. He jammed the shotgun against my sternum.

The air in my lungs went ice cold, and I pulled away from the hard metal.

Steady. Keep moving. I couldn't let him see me shaking. I deliberately slid my hand over to the twenties and pulled those two bills out. There weren't any tens. Three fives.

The sound of children's feet hopping down the ballroom stairs punctuated the robber's asthmatic breathing. I realized I'd been timing my movements to his raspy breaths. He stuck out his hand for the bag, and I flung it over the counter.

He cracked open the gun and shoved it inside his coat, scooped up the bag, and ran. If the gun wasn't loaded, I was going to be furious. He hit the glass doors, shoved them open, and took off through the park with an odd lope that covered ground in a hurry, his coat flapping behind him. I followed to the doors and watched until he disappeared.

I turned around to find a family huddled together, the mom and dad shielding two little boys.

"Was that a—" The dad looked down at his young sons. I realized he didn't want to say the word out loud. "Are you all right? Are you going to call the police?"

I nodded. "But they won't be able to respond right away. They're busy with a search and rescue operation. Besides, he got what he came for, so he won't be back." I pointed toward the parking lot. "Is that your blue car?"

The man nodded.

"I'll go out with you, make sure you're safe."

The notion was laughable—that I could protect them—but the couple seemed reassured. They took their children by the hand and walked to their car. I observed the ritual buckling into car seats and waved as they backed out of the parking spot and left.

I locked the museum doors behind me and checked the tally list. Five out meant the museum should be empty now.

I thought through what I would need to tell Sheriff Marge. The man must have paid admission. Seven-fifty to steal about sixty dollars. I giggled. I looked at the cash drawer. The quarters, dimes, and nickels were still in their compartments.

My giggling increased, bordering on hysteria. Why had he done it? Maybe the aftershave meant he was on his way to meet his sweetheart after he knocked over the museum. Would the chosen lady be impressed? I dropped to the floor under the open drawer and laughed until my diaphragm ached.

Sheriff Marge didn't believe me.

"When was the last time I called in a false report?" I asked, all traces of humor gone.

"How about last night? You were clearly woozy. Any chance you imagined it?"

"What? No. What are you saying?"

Sheriff Marge sighed. "I'm saying we're at the second spot Henry identified from the air, and we've still got nothing."

I closed my eyes. Finding nothing was good, wasn't it?

"I'm sorry. I shouldn't have said that," Sheriff Marge said. "Give me the guy's description again."

I complied.

"No vehicle?"

"Not in sight."

"Witnesses? Other than you?"

"Yeah, but I let them go. They had two little kids and were visibly frightened."

"Maybe they noticed something you didn't."

"I doubt it."

I was too tired to argue further. I hung up and sniffed—the lingering Altoids-on-steroids aftershave scent had revived my headache.

I collected my flashlight and thermos of stale coffee from the bathroom upstairs. My chin had had no effect on the doorknob, and the floor looked pretty clean. I closed the door and returned the pillow to the bed.

The chamber pot display was still in order—every pot in its place.

I called Mac. "Hey, have you seen Ford lately?"

"Yeah, he's sitting here at the bar, drinking a Dr Pepper."

"He told me the plumbing at his place is backed up. Could I ask you for a huge favor?"

"Anything." Mac really is a good man.

"I'm not sure he can do much cooking or washing at his place without the drains working right. Could you invite him to stay with you, maybe, and feed him until Rupert gets back and deals with the problem? I know it's a huge request. The museum trust fund will reimburse you."

"Nah, it's fine. I have an old army cot he can use. He told me he knows how to make squirrel stew, so maybe we'll have some."

"Are you serious?"

"Maybe." Mac laughed. "It's fine, really. How're you doing?"

"Waiting."

"I hear you. Take care."

When I drove up to my trailer, Tuppence didn't appear. She always emerges from her kennel or comes loping in from wherever she's been exploring. I called her. And called again.

Shuffling noises came from under the trailer, then a lonesome wail, like the end of a howl. I knelt and peered into the gloomy shadow. I could just make out the white parts of the dog's body. Tuppence swished the tip of her tail.

"Come out of there. What are you doing?"

Tuppence kept wagging but didn't budge. She whined.

"Are you stuck?"

More whining.

"Oh, for goodness' sake." I grabbed the flashlight and aimed it at the dog. Two pairs of eyes looked back—Tuppence's and a smaller set up between the wheels.

"Oh. Who did you find? Not everyone thinks your overtures are friendly, Tupp."

I wished I had one of those boards on casters for sliding under cars. I lay down and inched under the trailer by lifting and sliding my shoulders a couple of inches, then my butt a couple of inches, over and over again, using my feet for propulsion. Not unlike those horrible spongy green caterpillars with yawning mandibles that hump in the middle, then fling their front end forward. Hump—fling. Hump—fling.

Do you ever stop and think, I can't be doing this—not really—?

I was sick with worry about my missing intern, I'd witnessed the kidnapping/bashing/possible drowning of a young man who might be my intern, and I'd been robbed at gunpoint. But it took worming under an RV to free an unknown animal from the misplaced enthusiasm of my dog to make me think my life might be surreal. Or a nightmare.

"It had better not be a skunk, a raccoon, or a possum, or we're all going to stink to high heaven," I scolded, and wiped cobwebs off my face.

By now Tuppence was wagging violently and shivering with excitement.

I scooted into a better position and aimed the flashlight again. It had orange-and-white fur, which ruled out the wildlife I most dreaded. It was also rumbling.

At first I thought I'd left something motorized running in the RV. But I hadn't started the dishwasher, and I was pretty sure the fridge wasn't that loud. The rumble developed a little squeak, like a ball bearing out of place, and I realized it was a cat.

I wiggled my finger in the air to see if the cat would take a swipe. I didn't fancy the idea of a clawing cat fight in this tight space. No reaction. The purring continued.

Slowly I brought my hand toward the cat until it poked its nose out for a quick sniff. If anything, it was squeakier now. I was trying to work out how to get my hand around to grab the cat's scruff when it hopped onto my chest, wrapped its tail around tiny feet, and kept right on purring.

Tuppence was practically hyperventilating, and scrabbled closer.

I pushed her away. "Don't scare it now."

I rubbed the cat's cheeks, and the cat pushed back, eyes squinting in pleasure. I scootched out, holding the little creature in place.

Once free of the trailer, I sat up and cradled the cat in my arms. It was scrawny underneath mangy fur.

"Not eaten in a while, have you? Well, I think I have a can of tuna."

I kept the purring cat in a football tuck while awkwardly opening the can. I dumped tuna on a plate and let the cat eat on the counter, since Tuppence was frantic with anticipation.

"Go lie down," I told the dog. Tuppence reluctantly obeyed.

When the cat finished cleaning its whiskers, I carried it to the living room and set it on the floor in front of Tuppence, but kept my hands cupped around the cat just in case.

"Okay, let's see if you can be friends."

Tuppence nosed the cat, which let out a tiny hiss. It stalked away on stiff legs, back arched, then returned and repeated the hiss-and-stalk.

"You silly. You're taunting the poor old dog."

Tuppence whined.

"Yep, have at it, Tupp, but if you get clawed, it's your fault."

Tuppence stood and nosed the cat again. It immediately dropped to the ground and rolled over, using its back feet to kick Tuppence away. Then the cat walked straight underneath the dog and wound around her legs, purring, while Tuppence dodged her head every which way trying to keep an eye on it.

I laughed. "What should we name him? Should he be Tommy to your Tuppence, partners in crime-solving and mischief-making?" And so it was.

I called Sheriff Marge, promising myself it would be the last time today. Day seven was almost over.

"Still nothing," Sheriff Marge said, "but you should see the hordes of boats on the river, poking along the banks. Fishermen with lanterns. Word's spread that the drowning victim might be Bard Joseph, and people are out searching as though they expect a reward for finding him."

"But Julian hasn't offered one, has he?"

"No. Julian has sense."

"How is he?"

"Gone home. Hoping Bard'll drive up to the house and yell, 'I'm home.' Same way you're hoping Greg'll come walking out of the woods and say, 'Oh, I felt like going camping.'"

"What are you hoping?"

"I don't hope in these situations. I just deal with the facts. And there are so few of those my hands are practically tied. A body would be a fact, but I'm not hoping for that."

"What about my robber? I'm worried that when he realizes how little he got, he'll try again somewhere else. It could get ugly."

"I had Nadine call all the retail establishments along State Route 14 to tell them to watch out for a guy with funny teeth, a John Deere hat, and a coat big enough to hide a break-action shotgun. Most store owners are packing, too. They'll be vigilant."

"So he picked one of the few places with a cash register and no gun behind the counter. Maybe he's not as dumb as he looks."

"Maybe not."

CHAPTER 15

Loud ringing jolted me awake. I smacked the snooze button on the alarm. It kept ringing. Sunday—I'd semi-promised Pastor Mort that I would go to church. Maybe that's why he was calling me. Calling. The ringing.

I sat up and patted the blankets, feeling for my phone. The ringing stopped. I flipped on the light and peeled back bedding layers. I'd kicked my phone off the end of the bed, and it was trapped where the top sheet tucked under the mattress. I checked caller ID and dialed back immediately.

"Sorry. I was asleep."

"There's a body," Sheriff Marge said.

I moaned and sank onto the bed. "Who?"

"Don't know. He fits the basic description for both Greg and Bard. We need to go identify him."

"We?"

"Yes. You're the best person to give a positive ID if it's Greg. I'm calling Julian next. Want a ride? I'll pick you up in twenty minutes."

I pulled on a wool skirt, tights, and Mary Jane flats, then a long-sleeved cotton T-shirt and a warm cabled sweater. Identifying the dead seemed something to dress up for, out of respect.

I stepped down into the kitchen, headed straight for the coffee maker, loaded it, and pushed the start button. Maybe Sheriff Marge would need a mug, too.

Tuppence looked as though she wanted to get up, but Tommy was curled against her side just behind her front legs.

"Since I don't have a litter box, you'll both have to enjoy the outdoors today. If Tommy's still here when I get back, I'll work out some permanent arrangements, okay?" I scratched behind Tuppence's ears.

My mind was startlingly clear, as though it refused to acknowledge what I feared most and instead focused exclusively on mundane activities. It could be Greg's body several miles downriver—I knew it, but I didn't feel it yet.

Basic maintenance. How could life be normal with a dead body on a riverbank? I supposed weeping paralysis would come later, but for now I was numb and scarily efficient. Maybe I should call Pastor Mort.

Sally answered the phone. It was early, but Sally had a clear, cheerful voice not rusted by sleep.

I kept my tone detached as I explained. I didn't sound like myself at all. "I just wanted to tell someone. I don't suppose it can be announced publicly until we know who it is, next of kin and all that."

"I understand," Sally said. "We'll be praying for you and Julian."

"Does Julian go to church?" He'd mentioned God the day before.

"Not often, but he and Mort have long talks sometimes. Julian's a private man." That's what Sheriff Marge had said. "I'll bring a casserole over later." Food can be balm for the soul. If it included cheese, it just might work, for a little while.

I sighed. "Thanks. Oh, how's Paulina?"

"Just fine." Sally chuckled. "Her usual exuberance returned, and she bounced in the backseat of the bus the entire ride back to school. I didn't hear any of the other kids teasing her. I think they're a little awed by her experience."

I poured coffee into two travel mugs and doctored mine with milk and sugar, but left the other black for Sheriff Marge. A vehicle squealed to a stop outside. I scooped up the drowsy cat and shooed Tuppence outside. After depositing Tommy in Tuppence's kennel, where he burrowed into the old blankets, purring, I dumped food into Tuppence's bowl. Tuppence was usually an indiscriminate gobbler, so there was no point in setting out food for Tommy unless he was going to defend his own cuisine. Which he didn't appear inclined to do at the moment.

A dash back inside for the mugs, and I climbed into the steamy, warm SUV. The defroster was going full blast.

"Here." I handed the black coffee over to Sheriff Marge.

"Thanks. That'll pin my eyelids open."

"Short night?"

"Long night. No sleep."

"How's Julian?"

"He'll meet us there."

"That didn't answer my question."

Sheriff Marge scowled. "Julian doesn't discuss his feelings with me. Was that a cat?"

"Yeah. Stray. Tuppence treed him, so to speak, under the trailer last night."

Sheriff Marge grunted.

"Can you tell me what you know?"

"Sure. Ironic in a way. The river is crazy with people who have no business being on it, acting like treasure hunters. Seems they forgot the body would move with the current if it wasn't snagged. So a guy with tribal fishing rights named George Longshoe, minding his own business, went out this morning to check his nets, and his boat quite literally bumped into a body floating several inches below the surface.

He towed it to shore and called 911. I talked to him. Sensible fellow, matter-of-fact. He's waiting for us, to give his statement."

State Route 14 wound through deep forest as we drove west. Wisps of fog hovered over the wet pavement and snaked through the trees. Every once in a while, glimpses of a much more dramatic river gorge emerged—plummeting cliffs, thick trees, fog shrouding a river that was deeper and narrower here, and moving at a crushing pace, not that you could tell from the surface.

We crossed the Columbia on the Hood River Bridge, which offered spectacular views in both directions on clear days.

Sheriff Marge drove east to a run-down riverside campground. It was full of what appeared to be squatters, but I guessed they were permanent residents. I hadn't realized so many other people had the same living arrangements I did, but this was a ghetto compared to my Fifth Avenue apartment.

Tarpaulins and sheets of plywood provided additional shelter and extended the living quarters outside old moss-covered trailers. Junk, the kind collected over a lifetime, lay scattered around and between the sites, much of it fishing related. Floats, traps, gasoline cans, propane stoves, hip waders, homemade smokers, broken lawn chairs.

We followed muddy ruts that ended at a boat ramp and a rickety dock. Sheriff Marge wedged the Explorer between an unmarked white van and a police cruiser. The fire department was there, and an ambulance.

I counted three more police vehicles and the dirty Explorer of the Wasco County Sheriff—Sheriff Marge's counterpart on the Oregon side. I wondered if county sheriffs got a bulk rate on SUV purchases. There were more functioning vehicles in the campground now than there had probably been in all its years before, combined.

A few dinghies and one skiff with an outboard motor bobbed along the dock. A cluster of uniformed people stood to the side of the dock—and beyond them, a blue tarp covered a prone ridge that was just over six feet long. The water lapped at arm's reach from the body as it lay on river rock and dark-green, algae-filmed mud.

"Okay. Give me a minute." Sheriff Marge stomped toward the group and said a few words, and everyone except Sheriff Marge turned to look at me.

I hadn't counted on having an audience for this ordeal. I stared at the ground. I was also wearing the wrong shoes. Mud oozed around the soft brown leather of my Mary Janes while I concentrated on breathing at a normal rate. In—out. In—out.

Sheriff Marge's thick-soled boots came into the picture. "I want to go ahead. Because if it's . . . well . . . then we can spare Julian."

I nodded.

I slipped and fought to stay upright as I followed Sheriff Marge across the muddy shore toward the blue tarp.

A pudgy man wearing blue rubber gloves squatted beside the tarp and squinted up at me. He wore glasses with thick black frames, the lenses blurred by a thin layer of condensation. He blinked. When I nodded, he pulled the corner of the tarp back.

Puffy white skin stretched over his nose and chin, and deep blue shadows beneath made him look old and weary. Dark hair was plastered in clumps over a bloodless gash on his forehead. His brown eyes stared at something far beyond me, and at nothing, almost sinking into midnight blue. It was a gaunt, cold version of the boy in Julian's photo. Bard did not have his father's eyes.

Sheriff Marge exhaled.

The tech replaced the tarp, and I shifted my gaze back to my shoes.

"I hate this." Sheriff Marge returned to the group of official people, leaving me to fend for myself.

I struggled up a low bank and sought shelter next to a clump of tall grass and a few volunteer saplings. I closed my eyes—still numb.

Julian would arrive in a few minutes. If he saw me, he'd know. It would be all over my face. Maybe that would be easier for him. Maybe I should go to him first.

A firm hand grasped my arm gently, just above the elbow, and stayed there, its warmth soaking through my sweater. I turned.

A thickset man about my height gazed at me with impenetrable black eyes. Deep lines from the sides of his nose to the corners of his mouth lengthened his dark-brown face. His salt-and-pepper hair was parted in the center and cut to his shoulders. He wore a denim shirt, jeans, and black rubber boots. The neck of a gray T-shirt peeked out above the top shirt button.

"I'm George Longshoe."

"Thank you, for all you did. For helping us know."

"You want hot tea?"

I ducked my head. "Very much. But I think I should stay until his father arrives."

"Of course. You're his mother?"

"No. I'm waiting for someone else to wash up."

George nodded as though that made sense.

"But I hope—" I wanted to explain that *my* person might still be alive—maybe.

The rumble of a diesel engine gearing down came from the mud track behind the parked vehicles.

I moaned, and George looked at me with increased concern. "His father," I said.

George eased my arm through his. "We'll meet him."

He led me over rough grassy ground so I didn't slip, and we faced Julian between two police cruisers before he could see the blue tarp.

Julian dipped the brim of his Stetson. "George."

"Julian." They clasped hands.

Julian looked at me. Those golden eyes plunged deep and found the answer. His face did not change. "Where is he?"

I held out my hand and he took it. The assembled officials hadn't noticed us yet. George accompanied us and did the honors of folding back the tarp.

"My son." The words were clenched, tight, and came from the back of Julian's throat.

George replaced the tarp. Julian stared out over the water, at the trees in their fall brilliance reflected in the little harbor's calm ripples. Out to the forested edges of the opposite bank. The fog had lifted. I squeezed his hand. He squeezed back and kept a tight grip.

I wanted to bury my face in his shoulder and cry for him, since his tears wouldn't come. But I couldn't fall apart. Not now. He was draining my strength—from my hand to his—and I couldn't let him down.

"Julian?" Sheriff Marge had come up quietly.

He shifted his gaze to her. "Yes." Then he said it again to answer the unspoken question.

"The medical examiner needs to speak with you."

Julian followed her.

George walked around the body and stood beside me. He studied the river with me, a solid, steady presence.

"You know him," I said.

"An acquaintance. He buys salmon from me every year, more than he can eat. He is a generous man. I never knew his son, or I would have handled this differently."

"You did right, George."

He turned toward me. "Right or good? But this is not the time to be philosophical." He placed his hands on the outsides of my shoulders. "I will pray that the one you seek will be found safe."

"Thank you," I whispered.

"Meredith." Sheriff Marge was back. "Take Julian home."

He was walking toward the parked cars, and I hurried to catch up with him.

"Do you trust me with your truck?" I asked, and held out my hand.

Julian flashed me a quick glance, fished in his pocket, and dropped the keys in my palm.

CHAPTER 16

I climbed into the driver's seat. It felt like a cockpit with all the dials and knobs and buttons, and it took me a while to adjust the seat so I could reach the pedals. Julian tried pointing to levers and things I needed, but his mind was clearly elsewhere. I found the ignition and did an eight-point turn without bashing into any of the shanty trailers. I slid it into drive and rolled up to the main road.

Now I understood what Julian had meant about the center console. I didn't really know this man, but I wanted to crawl over there into his lap and wrap my arms around him. Nothing romantic about it. He needed holding together. I'd never seen such quiet, penetrating distress—fissures running through that tough veneer.

I was supposed to be driving. The truck didn't have autopilot. I stared at the dashed yellow line as it flew under the left corner of the hood.

As I slowed to take the Platts Landing exit, Julian roused. "Please go to your house. I can drive the rest of the way on my own." He noticed my short grimace. "Is that all right with you?"

"Sure. It's just that, technically and figuratively, I live on the other side of the tracks. It's, uh, humble."

Julian snorted softly. “I do not care about that.”

“I know.” I shouldn’t have said it.

Mort and Sally’s minivan was parked in front of my truck and trailer. I brought Julian’s truck to a stop on the grass beside their van. I hoped Herb, my landlord, wouldn’t mind, just for a little while. He was picky about his grass.

Sally waved with one hand, casserole cradled in her other arm. Mort was holding Tommy up to his face, and they were rubbing cheeks while Tuppence happily sniffed the new pant legs. The cat was probably purring like a lawn mower.

“Will you stay?” I asked in a low voice, after I turned off the engine but before we made a move for the door handles. “I can’t eat that casserole all by myself.” I watched the shift happen, when Julian’s thoughts caught up with real time and the needs of the living. He drew a breath, gazed at me for several seconds, and nodded.

Should I have placed a demand on him that way? So soon? Mort and Sally were waiting. I nodded back and hopped out of the truck.

“We were just leaving a note,” Sally said.

“And trying to figure out a place to put the casserole where Tuppence couldn’t get into it. This little cat added a new wrinkle, since I assume it can climb?” Mort asked.

I tried to answer in the affirmative, but Sally was giving me a big, muffling hug.

“I’m very sorry,” I heard Mort say, and peeked over Sally’s shoulder to see him shaking Julian’s hand with both of his. So they knew.

“Will you do the service?” Julian asked.

“Of course. Of course I will.” Mort put his arm around Julian’s shoulders. He had to stretch up to do it, but he held the embrace for a manly few seconds.

“We’ve just come from the potluck,” Sally murmured to me. “I made two casseroles and saved this one for you. It could use a few minutes in the oven to reheat.”

I unlocked the trailer and ushered everyone, animals included, inside. I'd never had so many people in my RV before, but they all found a place to sit without too much trouble. Tommy made himself comfortable on Mort's lap.

"I think you brought dessert, too, didn't you, honey?" Mort asked.

"Yes, it's still in the cooler."

Mort handed Tommy to Julian and bustled out. Tommy's purring was audible from where I was leaning against the kitchen counter. I dumped a can of tuna on a plate and passed it to Julian. Tommy dug in.

"He showed up last night. I don't have all the trappings for a cat, so it's a good thing I do have a stash of canned tuna," I explained.

Sally helped me set out plates and silverware, and we all crammed around the dining table. Mort and Sally took modest helpings.

"We just ate a couple hours ago," Sally said.

"That doesn't matter, honey," Mort said. "You're the best cook in the world. Oh, you and Meredith are, I mean."

"I quite agree with you. Sally is the best." I helped myself to a steaming mound of chicken, peppers, and onions rolled in flour tortillas and smothered in a cheesy cream sauce, like enchiladas but better.

Julian didn't say anything, but he inhaled his food, which I took to be a good sign.

"I don't want to be pushy, but would it help to talk about it yet?" Mort asked.

I waited for Julian. The muscles in his jaw rippled again, as if he was restraining words until they could be measured.

"I expected it. I think I knew." He turned toward me. "I'm sorry you had to go through that today."

I shook my head. "I wanted to be there."

"He came home—my prodigal boy. He tried to seek shelter, but his past followed him." Julian pushed his Stetson back, rubbed his forehead, then resettled the hat. "I should have protected him more."

"Yet he was a man, and he made his own decisions. There are always consequences," Mort replied. "What-iffing will rob the usefulness from your life."

Julian nodded. "I know that well, but I think I need to ache for a while."

"Yes, you do. It is sometimes good to sense the magnitude of sin, the results of sin. Then we treasure salvation all the more."

I pondered in silence. Pain was good? Death was good? An example to the living to take heed? Some people seemed to get more examples than others, like Julian. A man of wealth, prestige—and deep sorrow.

Sally looked around at our somber faces. "Dessert?"

I ate the chocolate-cherry-something without appreciating it. I was suddenly leaden. My body moved at a sluggish pace, as though sleepwalking—my brain lagged even further behind, failing to give the right commands at the right times. Whatever spurt I'd had earlier, when Julian needed it, was gone now. Julian seemed to be suffering from the same malaise.

Mort and Sally kept up a conversation. The sound was distorted, as though filtered through the narrow end of a funnel. I knew I wasn't responding properly. I did manage to scoop half the remaining casserole and dessert into containers for Julian to take with him. He moved stiffly toward his truck, climbed in, nodded the Stetson, and drove off.

"I hope he makes it home," I murmured.

Mort heard me. "He will. We have yet to see the depths of his fortitude in God's grace, I think."

"Someday I'll know what you mean. I only get snippets now."

Mort looked a little embarrassed.

"No, no." I patted his arm. "I like it. How did you know—when we arrived? I couldn't think of a way to signal you."

"There was only one reason you'd be driving his truck."

ooo

Full stomach, warm fireplace, and a drowsy cat in my lap whose purring had tapered off to a minor vibration. Tuppence's heavy head rested on my right foot. This was how life was supposed to be. Sharp rapping at the door broke into my stupor. Had someone driven up? How long had I been dozing? Was it Julian?

I dumped Tommy, who hit the floor with a squeak. "Sorry," I whispered, and scrambled for the door.

A worn-out Sheriff Marge stood on the step. There was a new darkness under her eyes, and her skin had more wrinkles, as if she'd deflated a little.

"Come in," I said. "I have casserole."

"Of course you do. Sally?"

I nodded and popped a loaded plate in the microwave.

"This time I'll ask you. How's Julian?"

"He's hard to read. Mort says we haven't seen the depths of his fortitude in God's grace yet."

"I expect Mort's right." Sheriff Marge devoured the casserole. She pushed the plate away and sighed.

"Dessert?"

"No. I've got something else to tell you. I'm looking forward to the day when we'll be able to chat about potlucks and break-ins again, but right now I have more bad news."

I sat down.

"Pete Sills called. He was coming back empty from a trip upriver. You know those turnoffs along State Route 14 where the heritage trail markers are?"

"Yeah. There's a bunch of them. I went out to one on . . ." When was it? Ages ago. Less than a week ago. "Monday," I finished.

"At the first one east of Lupine, he noticed a large swath cut through the brush down the side of that steep bank into the river. Not a mudslide because the vegetation was still rooted in place, but like something large had crashed through it."

I waited, my body rigid.

"He anchored the tug and took the dinghy out to have a closer look. There's a light-colored car in the water below the parking spot. He couldn't tell make or model or exact color. It's too deep to see clearly." Sheriff Marge pressed her lips together. "It's getting dark, and the car's not going anywhere tonight, so I'm arranging for the dive team to come out first thing in the morning."

"Okay."

"You understand?"

"Yes."

"Can you think of any reason why Greg—and I'm not saying it's his car—would drive east last Sunday instead of west?"

I shook my head. "I drove by there on Monday, and I'm sure there weren't any cars at that marker, especially not Greg's."

"Okay." Sheriff Marge rubbed her large hands on her thighs as though she were trying to generate the energy to carry on. "Normally we don't let family watch or participate in the rescue efforts. We keep them a safe distance away to spare them. Julian was an exception because I knew he'd keep it together. You're an exception, too. You're not technically family, but you're closer to Greg than any of his real family. You can come if you want, but I'm reserving the right to send you home if I think it's best." She rose, and I watched her leave.

What I'd said to George about waiting for someone to wash up—that had been real, hadn't it? The words had just come out. And now they seemed prescient. I was going to have to do it again—identify a body. Was there any hope left?

I climbed into bed, my throat scratchy and my head pounding.

CHAPTER 17

I sat bolt upright, heaving air in through my mouth. My head felt too heavy to hold up, and my body ached as though it had come out on the losing end of a wrestling match.

I staggered into the bathroom and squinted at my bloodshot eyes in the mirror. A futile effort to blow my nose only exacerbated the headache. My sinuses felt clogged with cement. Lindsay's cold had caught up with me. Did we have Lysol at the museum? I wished I had thought to spray the entire gift shop.

My body plodded through getting-ready-for-the-day motions. It was still dark out, so hurrying wasn't necessary. Eventually I would need to think about what was coming, but if pain could be postponed—that seemed the better course. When it was necessary, I'd settle into the grief, like Julian, and devote time to it. Would it ever end?

I stood under the hot shower for a long time. The start of day nine. Maybe there was no longer a need to count.

It was easy to figure out which heritage trail marker Sheriff Marge had meant. The small gravel turnoff overflowed with emergency vehicles. They lined the edge of the highway before and after the marker. I parked past another pickup with a volunteer-firefighter sticker in the window and walked back to the scene of the action.

People swarmed all over the place. I recognized a few members of the dive team.

Pete's tug was anchored close in. Several ropes trailed into the water from the cliff above the river and from the tug's stern. I found Sheriff Marge talking with a fire captain.

"The cliff's too unstable here to winch the car up the side. Several members of the dive team are on their way out to Pete's tug, which they'll use as their base. Pete has several winches and all the cable they'll need." Sheriff Marge shielded her eyes from the rising sun. "These guys hold down other jobs. We'll try to get this done quickly so they can still work most of a normal day."

I sneezed—a debilitating explosion.

Sheriff Marge stepped back. "You look terrible." She squinted. "I can't afford to have any of my crew get sick. Stay out of the way and keep your germs to yourself."

Mindful of Sheriff Marge's no-family-present lecture, I retreated to the heritage marker and sat on a boulder directly behind, facing the river. Today no one read the sign—no one cared about the animal life Meriwether Lewis had noted in his journal in funny, misspelled English, like Adam naming creatures he'd never seen before. And I didn't want to be sent home. I had to be present when Greg was found, no matter what condition he was in, or I was in.

Pete's red buffalo plaid jacket stood out against the tug's white paint. He caught the line a dive team member tossed and eased their boat alongside, securing it to the railing. The divers hoisted gear and oxygen tanks onto the tug.

No fog today. Long golden light shafts stretched over sagebrush hills. The breeze picked up, buffeting my plugged ears. I wished I'd worn a hat. I bypassed my nose and took in cold gasps of air through my mouth. Cupping my hands over my ears, I concentrated on the tug, abdominal muscles tight against involuntary shivering.

Sunlight glinted off the windows, and spray sloshed over the deck when the river's chop hit the stationary bow. The water was rough for a rescue operation, but everyone seemed to have an urgency today, even the emergency responders for whom this kind of thing was normal.

The dive team suited up. Two men jumped into the river off the stern, bobbed to the surface, and spent a few minutes adjusting their equipment. Crew members on deck spooled out the now-familiar yellow nylon rope.

The divers pushed off, one after the other. Their heads and oxygen tanks bobbed between waves as they kicked toward shore. They stopped to confer about ten yards out, then submerged. I held my breath.

Deputies, firefighters, EMTs, dive-team members—everyone—lined up at the edge of the cliff and peered into the river. I shifted forward with them, but maintained quarantine. I couldn't stop shivering.

The divers were under for fifteen, twenty minutes. No bubbles surfaced. Eddies turned on one another against the rocks at the base of the cliff. The silt-filled water frothed, almost cappuccino in color. How could they see anything?

I blinked to relieve my burning eyes. The wind whipped around me, molding my jacket to my body, so I turned slightly to present a narrower profile. Pete leaned against the tug's railing, binoculars raised to his eyes. He wasn't looking at the base of the cliff or the crowd of people lining the ridge. He lowered the binoculars.

Maybe he'd been looking at me. With trembling hands I pulled my jacket collar up and hunkered into it, feeling far too gross and worried to be having romantic thoughts about that man. He could do whatever he liked with his spare time. But I was grateful for his help. He didn't have to be doing this.

The crowd shifted, murmured. I caught their voices on the wind and looked quickly at the water. One diver was up. He gave a thumbs-down gesture to the crowd. They responded by easing away from the edge.

Heedless of germs, I pushed through the group toward Sheriff Marge.

Sheriff Marge shook her head when she saw me. "No body. They're going to pull the car out now." She waved me back, out of the way.

No body. No body. Was the car even Greg's? Anger against Greg swelled in my chest for the first time. Where had he gone? Why hadn't he said something? Maybe he was off cavorting, as Mac had suggested. I returned to my boulder and hunched against the wind.

The divers towed hooks attached to cables from the tug to the car. They submerged but weren't gone as long this time. They cleared the area and signaled the tug.

Pete operated the winches, slowly pulling the cables tight. Nothing seemed to happen. The winch motors ground on, the sound whining unevenly across the water.

I strained to hear metal scraping over rocks as the car was pulled out of its resting spot, but the water dampened whatever sound there would have been, and the wind howled over the top of the cliff. Weak sunlight filtered pale through horsetail cirrus clouds.

Two wheels and part of a back bumper came to the surface at the tug's stern. Pete turned off the winches and strapped the car to the tug with the help of the divers. The car was upside down, but the stubby rear end looked like a Prius's.

Pete held his hand to his ear. He was calling someone. I sought out Sheriff Marge in the crowd. She was also talking on her phone.

I sprinted in her direction, but only for a few seconds until lack of oxygen forced me to double over in a coughing fit. I'd used up all the Kleenexes in my pockets. Sheriff Marge was beside me when I finally stopped hacking.

"It's Greg's car. The license plate matches."

"You're sure there's no body?" I croaked.

"Yeah. All the windows are closed, so he didn't get out that way. We'll pull the car onshore and check the trunk."

I swallowed. I hadn't thought of that. Greg dead in the trunk. That would be no accident, except—"I don't think his car really has a trunk. More of a hatchback cargo area."

"We'll go over every inch of the car. Go home and go to bed. I'll call you."

I made it home with no memory of the drive. My head floated in its own separate bubble, and I ached all over, especially in my ear canals. Tuppence met me, but Tommy was notably absent.

"Where's your friend?" I rasped, but Tuppence just wagged.

Two hours later my phone rang. Sheriff Marge said, "Contents of Greg's car: one duffel bag with assorted clothes and toiletries, part of a case of water bottles, the usual jack, tire iron, and jumper cables, insurance papers and maps in the glove box, some loose change, an air freshener hang tag, an MP3 player. The parking brake was not set."

"Ordinary stuff," I said. "Now what? Do you think it was an accident?"

"We're going to treat the heritage marker as Greg's last known location and assume he was moving on foot from there. We'll run another request for the public's help on the news channels tonight. I'm sending deputies out to canvass the next several towns east to find out if anyone saw him going in that direction. He may have been disoriented, especially if he saw or caused his car to go over the edge. We'll check at the truck stops—maybe he was hitchhiking. We've already searched the heritage marker parking lot and didn't find anything we could link to him."

"It's not much, is it?"

"No. But at least we have a starting location. Very few people truly disappear without a trace. We'll find him."

"What can I do to help?"

"Nothing. Eat chicken soup. Sleep."

I didn't have a can of soup of any kind in the pantry. With no energy to make a grilled cheese sandwich and thinking I should save the last can of tuna for Tommy when or if he returned, I settled for some expired codeine-laced cough syrup. The thick, sweet liquid coated my tongue, slid down my throat, and warmed my belly. I curled up in a recliner and fell into a heavy sleep with my mouth open.

I snored myself awake. The LED clock on the microwave provided the only light in the trailer—3:52. A steady thrumming on the roof explained the early dusk. That kind of relentless rain fell from low, dark clouds draped over the hills. Quite a switch from this morning, but weather patterns sail through the gorge.

My throat was parched and sore. I got up for a glass of water and a second dose of cough syrup and its welcome oblivion.

But my brain was too busy to go back to sleep. Greg had left so few items or hints of personal interest behind. That was a clue in itself, wasn't it? He hadn't said anything to Betty. He hadn't seemed distressed. He'd eaten a normal breakfast. But he hadn't left anything in his room. Had he intended to return?

I pictured Greg's bare bedroom. The only things out of place were mine—the books Greg had borrowed, sitting on the chair. I inhaled as a thought hit me, prompting a painful coughing fit.

That day in my office, when Greg had borrowed the books, he'd cradled them in his arm. There was more thickness to that stack than to the pile of books I'd removed from the chair when I sat at his desk.

Backpack. Laptop. Phone. Those items had not been on Sheriff Marge's list of what was in Greg's car. Things you took with you when you traveled. Things you used to stay in touch. Greg hadn't meant to go missing. What had he been planning?

The missing book or books could be the answer.

"Come on, Tupp. You love Greg, don't you? Come with me." I needed the dog to bounce ideas off.

Tuppence wagged and pranced at the door.

Ignoring my rumbling stomach, I grabbed the flashlight and a wad of tissues. The codeine made me dizzy, but if I hung on to something for a minute, the world righted itself until I moved too fast and sent it spinning again. Nice and easy.

I went down the steps one at a time and followed Tuppence's white tail-tip beacon to the truck.

My brain could do only one thing at a time, so there was no further analysis while I steered the truck onto State Route 14 toward the museum. Oncoming headlights made huge, glaring halos on the rain-spattered windshield. I swerved away, caught sight of the white line, and brought the right wheels back inside the lane. Tuppence whined.

"I know, I know." My head pounded as though a giant fist were squeezing the base of my skull. If I hadn't needed my head to think, I wouldn't have minded being separated from the source of my misery.

I slowed to improve my chances of going straight. If that bothered anyone, they could just pass me. Wouldn't be hard to do. I coasted through the turn into the city park, down the slope, and into the museum parking lot.

Ford, swaddled in a bright-yellow rain slicker, was riding the big lawn mower through the trees, using the attachment to suck up soggy fallen leaves. The vacuum on that thing could probably inhale a bowling ball. He waved, but I needed both hands on the steering wheel. The big mower had headlights, but he'd still have to quit soon. The low clouds were creating a thick gloom. I thought the term was *socked in.*

The museum is closed Sundays and Mondays and seemed cavernous without the sparse but comforting human element. Tuppence's nails clicked on the oak parquet floor as she chased scents along the high baseboard molding and sneezed repeatedly to blow dust from her nose.

She trotted behind me through the dark rooms and into the waiting patron-friendly elevator. This one had carpet and wood paneling, unlike the utilitarian freight elevator, and I never used it. Except today, when every step required a rasping fight for air and my limbs shuffled instead of swung in their usual cadence.

I slid to the floor with my back against the walnut burl. Just a little rest while the elevator hummed to the third floor. A subtle ding and whoosh as the doors opened announced that it was time to exit. I rocked to my hands and knees and slowly stood. I hung on to the handrail for a few seconds until the floor became perpendicular to my point of view. My throat felt as though it had been scraped with sandpaper.

Tuppence loped along the hall and sat in front of my office door. I fumbled with the key until the lock jiggled loose. I let the dog in, flipped on the overhead light, and squeezed my eyes shut.

When I could render the overhead light tolerable by peeking through my lashes, I swung around to the corkboard on the back of the door and ripped Greg's borrowed book list from the thumbtack. Six books—two on Columbia River Gorge geology, one on regional Native American history, two on petroglyphs and rock art, and *The Journals of Lewis and Clark*.

"What are you up to, Greg?" I whispered.

Tuppence cocked her head.

"Back to the truck," I said, and Tuppence led the way.

A huge plop of water dropped down my collar as I stepped out of the museum. It trickled between my shoulder blades and soaked into my bra band. I shivered all over. My jacket was water-resistant but not waterproof. But I wasn't going back. Not now.

Tuppence was soaked, too, and left puddles on the seat as she scampered across to her place by the passenger window. I eased the truck into gear and drove slowly toward Betty's, almost missing her driveway in the dark, sheeting rain.

As I pulled up to the house, Betty's porch light came on, and her silhouette appeared in the kitchen doorway. That sixth sense. She'd probably made cookies.

"Honey, what are you doing out in this weather?" Betty called. She bent to pat Tuppence just as the dog launched a jowl-flapping shake, spraying water droplets over an extensive radius. Betty wiped her face on her apron.

"Sorry about that," I said.

"Not to worry, honey. I'm a farm girl, through and through. In fact, I should have given her a minute to make herself presentable before trying to pet her. Come in out of the wet."

Tuppence and I started steaming the moment we entered the warm kitchen. I sneezed onto my sleeve. Nice.

"Oh dear," Betty said. "How about some hot Tang? You need the vitamin C."

"I'd really love that, but I need to look in Greg's room again."

"Of course, dear. I'll get your Tang ready while you do that."

I stepped into Greg's room and went straight to the pile of books, still on the bed where I'd left them. Four books. I compared them to Greg's list. The petroglyph books were missing.

Petroglyphs. What was Greg searching for? Ancient artwork with spiritual or narrative meaning? A graduate student's dream. Something to impress Angie.

I returned to the kitchen and slid into a vinyl dinette chair. Betty pushed a warm mug into my hands. Neon-orange liquid swirled, releasing a pungent tangerine scent.

"Want a cookie?" Betty asked. "Chocolate and orange are good together."

I accepted a chocolate chip cookie, also warm—the chips still melty. "Mmm." I chased the cookie with the Tang and cringed. Still, it tasted better than cough syrup.

Tuppence flopped under Betty's chair for a cranium massage.

"What a sweet hound," Betty said.

"We need to get going. Thanks, Betty."

"You sure you can't stay? It's miserable out there."

"Yeah, we have things to do. I'll bring Tuppence back on a nice day, get a tour of your farm."

"I'd like that. You take care, now. Drive safely."

More like drive sober. I grimaced, reeling as I stood. A wave of dizziness and nausea washed over me. The sugar, citric acid, and codeine weren't playing well together. I staggered out the door to the truck. Betty didn't wave, but stood on the porch, arms folded across her chest.

Day nine. I had to snap out of this haze. Concentrate.

Greg had made a plan, and it involved petroglyphs at the heritage marker past Lupine. Maybe something would come to me if I stood in the same spot. Get inside his skin. What had he been thinking? I tossed the books onto the seat beside me, and Tuppence nosed them.

East toward Lupine on a dark and rainy Monday night. Two cars passed going west. The steady pounding rain and whoosh of road spray, the thump-click-thump of the windshield wipers, lulled me into a trance.

The third time my head snapped to attention—how long had I been dozing?—I turned on the radio. The public jazz station at Mt. Hood Community College was playing the Squirrel Nut Zippers. I tapped the steering wheel along with "Fat Cat Keeps Getting Fatter," which helped—for a couple of minutes.

I straightened up as we rolled into Lupine, the retail section of town closed for the night. A few lit signs splashed colorful reflections on the wet pavement. The tavern, with its flashing neon beer logos—some partially burned out—and surging white rope lights outlining the flat facade, had a packed parking lot. Mostly dented 4X4 rigs raised on knobby tires. One diehard had ridden his Harley into town and parked it in the dry patch under the small overhang sheltering the windowless door. Monday-night football viewing in the sticks.

And that was it. Lupine lasted four minutes. I turned the high beams on and peered through the rivulets streaming down the windshield for the heritage-marker turnoff. I found it more by feel than by sight, grateful for the crunch of gravel under the tires. I set the parking brake—hard—and got out.

The river was a dark abyss. I knew it was there, but I couldn't pick out any details between where I stood and a few lights winking through raindrops on the Oregon side. Tuppence's tags jingled beside me.

I clicked on the flashlight, targeted the heritage marker in its beam, and shuffled over to stand near the familiar boulder. My head swam, and I blinked to clear my vision.

Where would someone go if they were looking for petroglyphs?

Down.

Dams dramatically raised the level of the Columbia long after the petroglyphs were carved into basalt by Native Americans who fished the river and established a thriving trading post here. The Dalles Dam submerged Celilo Falls, making this section of the Columbia traversable by boat. The white people's towns were relocated to safety when the dams were built from the New Deal through the 1950s.

Along the way a few forward-thinkers and history buffs had saved a smattering of petroglyphs by chipping them out and removing the rock slabs ahead of the rising water, but most were submerged and probably eroded beyond recognition. Documented eyewitness history lost to the thirst for increased commerce.

"What do you think, old girl?" I asked.

Tuppence bumped my leg with her nose and snorted.

"He's not going to make it if we don't find him soon. He might not—"

Tuppence whined.

"I know. Not yet." I wiped water out of my eyes. "I can't think that yet."

Where would a curious graduate student go looking for petroglyphs?

Down.

CHAPTER 18

I played the flashlight over the cliff edge. Short of falling, there appeared to be no way to get down to the river.

"Well, girl, where is he? Go find Greg."

Tuppence wagged and snorted but stuck to my side.

Should I wait for daylight and assistance? I patted the cell phone in my pocket. This was just a whim, a hunch at best—not worth bothering Sheriff Marge about. But Greg didn't have much waiting time left, if any. Nope—now or never. I wasn't going to let him down again.

I turned left and cut wide swaths with the flashlight as I crept along the edge. A couple of stones dropped and plinked against the cliffside as they tumbled down. Steady. I passed the spot where Greg's car had gone over. Then my feet fell on rough turf—the end of the gravel parking area.

Tuppence trotted ahead around a knoll, nose skimming an inch off the ground. She made her usual hoovering sounds.

"That's right, old girl. Go find him."

I bumped into the dog's back end, and Tuppence yelped.

"Sorry. Why'd you stop?" I ran the light beam along Tuppence's back to her head and saw what she was sniffing—a crumpled Kentucky Fried Chicken bucket.

"No distractions, not tonight." I nudged Tuppence, then walked around the dog when she didn't budge.

The ground sloped downward at a mild grade from the heritage-marker viewpoint. Boulders left behind by thousands of years of erosion loomed at odd angles. I didn't know where I was going, but I kept my feet heading downhill. That meant squeezing between two boulders and taking a sharp turn to the right.

The ground was rutted into a channel caused by spring runoff. I needed to follow the trail of water, from small to big as gravity collected it into growing flows.

The rain had slowed to a drizzle, but I was beyond soaked. Tuppence caught up, and we slogged through mud.

I panned the flashlight ahead, taking my eyes off the ground for one second, and slid down a short embankment, landing hard on my rump with a gooshing, kissing sound in the sticky mud. Tuppence stuck a wet nose in my ear.

"I know. If I had four legs, I'd be better at this."

As I picked myself up, the flashlight beam wavered over the way we'd come, and I realized we'd been making switchbacks down large steps that marked separate lava flows from ages past. Over the years dirt had blown or been washed into crevices and corners of the steps. Grass rooted and held it there, creating ramps or slides from one level to the next. If I'd been able to see the whole thing from the start, I probably would have made the entire descent on my backside.

The river lapped against the bank below, but it was at least one more thick lava layer down. My sinuses ached, and my hands shook like I had three-espresso jitters, making the light beam bounce all over. Was it because I was cold and wet or because the codeine was wearing off? Codeine was supposed to be slept off, not used to mask physical ailments while one launched an ill-advised search. I tried to sigh but couldn't breathe that deeply. I coughed instead. My ears crackled.

Tuppence shuffled forward, nose to ground. She disappeared around a rocky outcropping. Then she sneezed and I followed.

Tumbled rocks blocked a narrow chasm—probably the remnants of an old rock slide. The exposed fronts of the lava shelves were vertically striated into eerie columns created as the lava had cooled. This chasm looked as though a crack had formed between columns, or maybe it had been there all along—maybe something deep in the shelf had created a wedge the lava flowed around. I'm no geologist, but that's my best guess. The next shelf up formed a ceiling of sorts, back in behind loose rocks. Tuppence was on top of the rock pile, waiting for me.

"You want to go back there?"

Wag wag.

"That's up, not down."

Wag wag. Shnuffle.

"Your scorecard is pathetic lately. Rodents, bullfrogs, one cat, and a KFC bucket."

Snort. Tuppence descended the rock pile on the other side, tail in the air.

"Gonna leave me behind, huh?" I muttered. My throat hurt.

Tuppence made it look easy, but I weigh twice as much and am half as nimble. I shoved the flashlight in my back pocket and felt my way forward on the pile. I shifted on chunks, seeking footing while grabbing for something sturdier ahead. A rock the size of a softball caromed off my thigh before nicking my opposite calf as it fell.

"Ugh."

Then whatever I was hanging on to with my left hand let go and I slid, scraping a raw streak into my palm and forearm. I lay panting at the bottom, grateful for the codeine's residual pain-killing effects.

Tuppence whined from the other side.

"I'm coming," I said, but I still lay there for a few minutes, waiting for my sight to return to single vision. A nap would be nice.

No. No, no, no. No nap. Besides, the flashlight lump under my right hip was not comfy.

I rolled over and crawled toward the wall. Maybe the side of the rock pile would be easier. My hands pressed against the basalt columns, finding grips in their crevassed surface. I inched sideways, like a crab, leaning on the wall for support when the rocks shifted underneath. Baby steps in the dark.

Shrubbery scratched my face. Hardy bushes clinging to the cliffside. I grasped a branch, tugged, found it firmly rooted, and pulled myself up, hand over hand, until my feet skiffed over the pile's rounded peak.

My shoulders felt as though they were being pulled out of their sockets. It's awfully hard to breathe when you're hanging from a branch, when your esophagus is jammed into your lungs even though you're stretched to twice your normal length. It just doesn't work, so I let go. I have a little extra backside, so losing some of it in the slide won't be a long-term problem. It hurt like crazy, though, regardless of codeine.

Tuppence whined and licked my chin. Then she head-butted my side.

"Yep. All right." I felt around to my back pocket and pulled out the flashlight. It clicked on instantly. Thank you, Maglite.

Tuppence wheeled and headed into the chasm. I looked back at the rock pile for a second, but we'd come too far to give up now. With my right hand against the basalt wall and my left holding the flashlight, I followed.

Rocky debris littered the path, forcing me to examine every step. The uneven ground separated between narrow fissures. I tried not to step on the cracks. A plunking staccato sound—water dripped into puddles, which then leaked into ragged cracks.

Water—fresh water—was leaking through the lava layers. I remembered the threes. Three minutes without air, three days without water, three weeks without food. The running rainwater was an excellent sign and spurred me on.

But it was rough going, my breathing raspy and fingertips raw from feeling forward along the rock wall. Even Tuppence stumbled, emitting soft grunts. I wondered if they made head lamps for dogs.

Tuppence sneezed, and the noise echoed at odd angles toward us and away. But that could have been my ears. They were still plugged and returning my own dampened heartbeat.

What was that?

Tuppence cocked her head, too, lifting her long, floppy ears as much as she could. We both froze, not breathing.

Gone. It was gone.

The chasm narrowed unevenly to a slit. The ground dropped away, too. We were going down again. Tuppence barged into the opening, then stopped, her back end blocking the bottom half.

"What's in there, Tupp?"

I aimed the flashlight over the dog's head. More rock—a dark void.

"Come on, let me through." I pulled on Tuppence's tail, and she backed out.

I squeezed into the channel, keeping my flashlight hand ahead. I stepped on something that cracked under my weight. Glass and plastic shards reflected in the flashlight beam. With my foot I scooted the pieces behind me, then I slid out of the channel and knelt to examine them. Tuppence stuck her nose in, too, and wagged her whole body.

Gray lenses and cobalt-blue frames. Sunglasses. The ones Greg wore had blue frames.

Last summer when we'd gone out to check the lighting for the museum's sign at the park entrance, Greg had switched to prescription sunglasses. He'd told me he knew about wiring, but we couldn't find the fuse box, and I wasn't about to let him fiddle with the connections while they were live. He'd shoved the sunglasses up on his head while peering under the sign. I'd realized he must be nearsighted.

Yeah, the sunglasses were his, or just like his. It would have been easy for them to fall off his head or out of a loose pocket while he was shimmying through. He was skinny, but those long limbs would have to have been folded awkwardly.

Tuppence snorted.

"You were right," I said. "He's close."

Close. My heart jumped into overdrive. Could he hear us? Time to holler.

I crawled over to the opening and pressed in as far as my shoulders allowed.

"Greg!"

Echoes.

"Greg!"

Was that a moan? The same sound as before, soft and distant. Could be anything.

There was one way to find out. If Greg could get in there, so could I.

The last time I'd had a choice, I'd chickened out and a dead man had been pulled from the water. I was going in.

But I was going to call the cavalry first. I backed out of the cavern, picking out spots where I'd stepped before. Suddenly there was a ticking clock in my head. Now that I knew Greg was in the cavern, I had to reach him, and fast. Maybe just knowing help was on the way would give him the strength to hang on.

I called Sheriff Marge. No answer. Unusual, but not unheard of. I left a message and, on second thought, set my phone on a boulder at the base of the rock pile. It wouldn't get a signal in the cave and maybe it had one of those GPS tracker things. I didn't know for sure. Still, the phone would do more good out here than inside. I ducked back into the cavern and scrabbled to the narrow chasm.

The opening was widest at the bottom. But not wide enough for my shoulders to pass through. If I lay on my side, I could wriggle past.

"You stay here," I told Tuppence.

The loose stones were sharp, like shards chipped off the walls. They cut into my skin as my jacket rode up. I squirmed, propelling my body through the opening. A sideways inchworm maneuver.

I sat on my haunches in the second room of the cave and tried to catch my breath.

Tuppence whined through the crevice.

"No, you stay."

The words caught in my throat, and I coughed until my eyes watered. The codeine had definitely worn off.

I panned the flashlight around the small chamber. Cracks as wide as my hand crisscrossed the floor. Rapid water drops spattered into an unseen puddle. I touched the glistening wall. Water ran in rivulets down the basalt. Freshwater. Puddles. Still the best news I'd had in a week.

"Greg!" I yelled.

Only my own voice came back, bouncing off the hard surfaces.

Then a shuffle, or a grunt—and it wasn't Tuppence.

But the dog whined in reply.

"You stay," I reminded the hound.

The largest crack in the floor extended up the wall on the far side of the chamber. I straddled the fissure and crawled toward the opening. I aimed the flashlight beam between its jagged edges. A wide-eyed owl stared back.

I screeched. The owl didn't blink.

It took a few seconds to realize it was the most gorgeous petroglyph I'd ever seen. Perfect, clean design. At least two feet tall. White lines chipped with precision into dark-gray basalt. I had to get through the crack.

CHAPTER 19

I wondered what Greg had thought when he saw the owl. Spectacular. Amazing. And worth every scrape and bruise. He must have been so excited. On the scent of a great discovery, his eyelids and toes tingling with anticipation—because that's how I felt. No wonder he'd pressed on.

The crack was a foot wide, maybe. I pulled off my jacket—forgot all about the cold and that I was already shivering like a naked Inuit. Adrenaline buzzed in my ears. Most of me is pretty squishy, so I thought I could make it. Your skeleton is actually a lot smaller than you probably think it is.

The crack in the floor was a problem. I stretched my arm down into it but couldn't feel the bottom. I'd have to go through sideways without anything to stand on. Since I'd need both my hands, I stuffed the flashlight in my back pocket again.

I crooked my right arm into the owl room, feeling for the wall. The crack was like a narrow hallway entering a larger chamber. I had to angle around a ninety-degree corner but figured I could hug it.

I swung my right leg through space and wrapped it around the corner, probing for a toehold. There—a little cleft. I pressed my weight into it. Rock-climbing lessons would have been helpful, if only I'd taken them at some point in my past, which I hadn't.

Free of the crack, I balanced on my toes, clinging to the wall of the petroglyph room like a bat. The cavern felt large—the way sounds bounced back to me had shifted. The echoes took longer. There had to be a ledge or something. Greg had made it through. So could I.

But I couldn't go anywhere without seeing. I leaned into the wall and let go with my right hand to reach for the flashlight. That's when the sneeze came.

As the tingling sprang up in my nose, I lunged to resume my grip—too late.

I somersaulted until my shoulder slammed into the cavern's floor. The flashlight clattered after me, swinging its beam around like a spastic strobe light.

Pain flashed through my body, and I drowned in it. I couldn't breathe. My brain screamed when I thought about breathing. Maybe I was screaming. No, my lungs were flat. I couldn't scream.

CHAPTER 20

I awoke later—hours, minutes? Groggy and bone-cold, I lay perfectly still in the darkness, taking inventory of my body parts. Swallowing tiny sips of air—focusing on the slight rise and fall of my chest and the stabbing pain each breath brought.

My shoulder throbbed. My neck throbbed. My head throbbed. Must have knocked it on the way down. The second concussion in a week.

My legs were twisted uncomfortably. I slowly stretched my quads and calves, wiggled my toes, bent and unbent my knees. All there. Not paralyzed.

I was going to be stiff if I didn't move. The flashlight lay several feet away, still on. My eyes fastened on the round dot of light it projected as I pushed up to a sitting position. Pain sliced through my right side from shoulder to hip. I clenched my teeth against a scream and wheezed in short breaths.

My eyes rolled back.

Focus. Focus on the light. Not a good time to pass out.

Pressing my left palm against a wall, I pulled my legs under me, squatted, then rose, teetering, to my feet. My right hand worked, but something was terribly wrong with my shoulder.

Grimacing—and using my left hand—I pushed my right hand into my front jeans pocket to take the weight off my shoulder.

I stumbled toward the flashlight. A grunt escaped as I bent to pick it up.

I leaned against the cool wall and forced shallow breaths. Sweat trickled behind my ears. If I held perfectly still, my brain seemed to have a little room for thoughts apart from the pain. Any movement brought sharp stabs—breath-stealing stabs.

I played the shaky flashlight beam around the walls.

The owl had friends. Lizards, a sun face, big-eyed goblins, a man with hairy legs, hard-shelled beetles, a cat-headed jellyfish. They probably had much more meaning than I could ascertain, and they danced over the walls.

"Wow." It came out as a croak. I squinted at each new carving as it appeared in the light. The Florence Accademia Gallery, but for petroglyphs—master versions with cruder student copies near them, squiggles that looked like doodles on a notepad, practice renditions that became progressively more sophisticated. Truly a treasure trove. And protected—for how many years?

Greg would have been ecstatic when he found this. But where was he?

I scanned the floor. A few scattered rocks along the edges, and a bat skeleton. I wrinkled my nose. From the pungent, stinky-sweet smell, I guessed there was also a fresh skunk carcass nearby.

The flashlight beam revealed a tennis shoe, then a jeans-clad leg. My breath caught, and I forced shallow panting to conquer the shooting pain in my side. I clenched my teeth and directed the beam up the body—belt, blue button-down shirt—Greg lying on his back, eyes closed, head at an odd angle.

I staggered to him, knelt, and laid a hand on his chest. My hand was trembling, but there was other movement underneath—barely. His ribs settled after a faint exhalation. I waited a long time for them to rise again.

"Greg?" I whispered.

Nothing.

"Greg?" Louder.

Nothing.

I pulled his eyelids back but didn't know what I was looking for. Didn't they do that on TV?

I examined the rest of his body. The denim around his left ankle was crusted with dried blood. I gingerly pulled the hem up and nearly passed out again. The leg above his ankle was fractured badly, the yellowish end of a bone sticking through scabbed-over skin.

Greg moaned, and I whirled to look at his face.

"Huhhnn." I clutched at my side and screwed my eyes shut—no sudden movements.

Greg was out, but he was still feeling at least some of the pain. That was good, right? That he could feel his leg? I carefully tucked the fabric over the break—he needed all possible protection.

His backpack lay on the ground within arm's reach. And several open plastic containers. I picked one up and sniffed. Sour, but with the sweet undertone of cream-cheese frosting. Greg had been eating my carrot cake. Surviving on my carrot cake. I counted containers. Four—so it was all gone.

One of my containers had a few tablespoons of water in it. He must have scooped some out of a puddle to drink. He'd kept his wits about him. Of course he would.

I rummaged through his pack—my books, his cracked laptop and dead cell phone. He'd pulled his pack with him through the opening above. And it had saved his life—so far.

Should I try to wake him? But what could I do for him now? Not much. Neither one of us could climb out of here.

"Oh, Greg. Why didn't you tell me?" I picked up his limp hand.

How long would we have to wait? I'd left my truck, phone, jacket, and dog as bread crumbs and given general directions for Sheriff Marge. It was hard to tell in the dark exactly where we were.

Tuppence wasn't very good at staying—she'd wander around. Someone would spot her, eventually.

I sat beside Greg and scooted his things into a pile to prop up the flashlight. I aimed the beam at the crack we'd come through so anyone peering through the first crevice would see it.

My stomach rumbled. Betty's cookie was long gone. I lay snug against Greg and flung my good arm over him, giving him what was left of my own body heat.

My shoulder and side knotted in throbbing spasms. But crying required energy I didn't have. I grabbed a fistful of Greg's shirt and whispered, "Hold on. Just hold on."

CHAPTER 21

I slept, fainted, had waking nightmares—I don't know. My mind flashed through a bizarre jumble of memories and keen sensations. Tommy was chewing on my ribs, which were exposed and bloody. I looked at them poking up out of my chest. I moved to push him off me, but my arm wouldn't work.

Clyde stuck his tongue out at Tommy, and the cat scampered away. Sheriff Marge shouted at Lindsay to sneeze into a pillowcase to keep the germs away from other people. And the robber with the stolen dentures brought me a towering carrot cake on a platter, fresh from my favorite Portland bakery.

"Nice and easy," Ford repeated as he pounded his fist on a transport cart. I shouted at him to stop that racket, but he ignored me.

My ex-fiancé told me to hold still while he tried to take my picture, but my long, wavy hair—the hair he preferred that took an hour and fifteen minutes to style every day—kept blowing in my face. Then the wind blew him off the cliff, and he fell into the river without a splash. He went straight to the bottom holding a yellow nylon rope.

Tuppence growled in my ear. Her breath smelled like licorice, and she pulled on my collar, dragging me—dragging me away from Greg.

"No!" I shouted. "No!

But no one listened.

George Longshoe served tea in tiny white plastic cups with tiny white plastic saucers while we huddled around a child-size table and balanced on tippy little chairs.

ooo

Bright light forced its way under my eyelids. I turned my head away and moaned. A squeaky wheel revolved underneath. I was riding the squeaky wheel, and I wanted off. I felt for Greg, but my hand clanked against a cold metal railing. I tried to sit up, and something heavy pushed me back.

"Greg?"

"Fine. He's going to be fine."

I knew that voice. Maybe. Everything was fuzzy and bright. And antiseptic. Angels don't wear antiseptic. And that robber guy—he was menthol.

ooo

Voices murmured, a buzz. A hive. A hive of owls. No, not a hive. A covey? Someone ratcheted tape off a roll. Scritchy sounds—around and around. They were packing me into a case for shipment with the chamber pots back to Germany. Well, that'd be nice. Maybe then I could sleep. I wanted the darkness of the cavern. I wanted Greg to be safe.

ooo

Someone was standing over me, breathing on me. I opened my eyes. Sheriff Marge.

"Ah, you're back," Sheriff Marge said.

"Where have I been?" My voice came out raspy.

"Hard to say, exactly. I'm still trying to figure it out myself. But it seems you visited Betty, then drove to the heritage marker, forged a trail to an unknown cavern, and cracked yourself up pretty badly on the rocks when you fell in. Sound familiar?"

I tried to swallow.

"Here, you're supposed to be sucking on these." Sheriff Marge placed a plastic cup in my left hand.

I tipped it to my lips and slid an ice cube into my mouth. "Where's Greg?" I asked around the frozen lump.

"In surgery. He won't be walking for a while, but the doctor says he can set the bone. He'll be okay. Don't worry." Sheriff Marge patted my good shoulder. "The guys had to pull his shirt off because you were hanging on to it for all you were worth. They let you keep the shirt and hauled Greg out first."

"Oh." I wrinkled my nose, embarrassed. "I hope I didn't hinder—"

"Nope. You were protecting him, if incoherently. Pretty voracious, considering the nature of your injuries."

I looked down. I was propped in a white bed, covered in white sheets, in the middle of a white room. I seemed padded.

"Broken collarbone, cracked ribs, concussion, mild hypothermia, severe dehydration—but that might be related to the sinus infection. You're amped up on antibiotics and morphine." Sheriff Marge gestured toward the tubes running into my arm.

"Oh." Boy, I was slow. My brain crept along. "How did you find us?"

"You didn't hear that crazy dog of yours howling her head off?" Sheriff Marge studied me over the tops of her reading glasses. "Well, first, Betty called. She thought you were acting unusual and was worried about whether you should drive. So we started looking for you. Wasn't hard to guess where you went. We found your truck at the heritage marker with its back bumper sticking out into the highway. Lousy parking job.

Confirmed Betty's suspicions about your ability to drive." Sheriff Marge paused and scrutinized me again. "We may talk about that later."

"Codeine," I mumbled.

Sheriff Marge raised one eyebrow.

"Cough syrup. I had some."

"Some?"

"I didn't measure."

Sheriff Marge sighed. "Found your footprints and skid marks on the slope. We almost bypassed that rock pile, thinking no one in their right mind would try to scale it. But Pete climbed partway up to have a look and took a tumble when Tuppence hit him in the chest. She just came flying over the heap and crashed into him."

"Pete?"

This earned another disapproving look from Sheriff Marge. "Wild horses couldn't have dragged him away. I think you and he need to settle some things."

I slid another ice cube in my mouth. "Did you get my message?"

"Yeah. After we found your phone. You must have called while I was divvying up leads with the state police, and I didn't notice until we saw your phone sitting there and figured out why you'd done that. Tuppence was carrying on with horrible, yippy howls, setting everyone's teeth on edge. She led us into the cave where we could see your jacket and broken sunglasses."

"Did you see the flashlight beam, through the next crevice?"

"Nope. There wasn't any light. We got firemen in there with big battery-powered light packs and jackhammers. Made the openings big enough to get them through with their gear. They rigged up some kind of sling. It took a community effort. There's a whole bunch of people waiting to see you, but the doc won't let them in yet. I claimed official privileges."

I managed a faint smile. "Did you see the petroglyphs? Greg found them."

"I didn't go in that far, but Pete was impressed."

"Pete?"

"Like I said, wild horses."

"They need to be protected from vandalism. And the Confederated Tribes should be notified. Can you—?" I shifted and gritted my teeth. The edges of things were getting fuzzy.

"Done." Sheriff Marge pressed a slender knob with a button on the end into my hand. "Here, click this if you need more painkiller."

I sighed and closed my eyes.

ooo

The bed jerked hard, sending painful light streaking behind my eyeballs. I groaned.

Someone had bumped the bed. I opened my eyes and saw a flash of red-and-black buffalo plaid.

Pete and his big feet. Pete in buffalo plaid and heavy boots.

"Sorry. Didn't mean to wake you," he said.

I gasped and remembered. I clutched the corner of his jacket, pulled it to my face and inhaled. Licorice.

"Mmm," I said into the rough cloth. I might have said some other stuff, too.

Pete unwrapped my fingers from his coat and held my hand in both of his. He rubbed his thumb across my knuckles.

What had I just said? Something loopy, no doubt, and hopefully slurred. Good grief. My face was stuck in a goofy smile as I slipped back into dreamy morphine land. I was probably drooling, too.

CHAPTER 22

A nurse with little Donald Ducks all over her tunic opened the blinds. "It's nice out. Thought we'd let in a little sunshine."

"Nice scrubs," I said.

The nurse laughed. "I usually work the pediatric ward, but my last patient went home an hour ago. I'm finishing my shift on this wing since it's pretty busy over here."

The room was more colorful now—vases of flowers covered the bedside table and shelf under the television. Carnations, lilies, sunflowers. Hard to believe it was almost winter.

"Do you know Greg Boykin? He's here with a broken leg."

"I was just in his room a few minutes ago. He's awake. Do you want to visit him?"

"Can I get out of bed?"

"Yep. Best thing for you. You need to start using those muscles. Let me get a robe and slippers."

The nurse propped me up, and I grimaced as I swung my legs over the side of the bed.

"Just take it easy. Go as slow as you want," the nurse said. She fitted slippers onto my feet and draped the robe over my shoulders like a cape. "Gotcha covered. No embarrassing gapes."

Lindsay appeared in the doorway with a bundle of freesia. "Hey, look who's up. Going somewhere?"

"To visit Greg."

"I'll go with you. I haven't seen him yet today."

I stood and wobbled.

"You have to take this with you," the nurse said, rolling the IV stand closer.

"I feel like a ninety-year-old with a walker," I grumbled. "You haven't seen him yet today? What day is it?"

"Wednesday. You pretty much slept through yesterday, but you look better today."

I hadn't thought about my appearance. But now that I was moving, I wasn't turning back to check myself in a mirror. Lindsay kept the turtle pace with me down the hallway.

Greg was propped up in bed, left leg resting on a foam wedge with a cast covering everything from the knee down. He was sipping apple juice.

"You look good. Better than last time I saw you," I said.

"My rescuer." Greg grinned.

"I didn't get you out. I just fell in with you." I eased into a chair, and Lindsay perched on the edge of Greg's bed. "How're you feeling?"

He chuckled. "To quote Ford, I got nothin' to complain about. And thanks for the carrot cake."

"I'll make you another if you'll tell me why you went off alone—without telling anyone."

Greg shook his head. "Lesson learned. Sheriff Marge already grilled me. I think she's miffed—and rightly so. I'm really sorry about the trouble and worry I put everyone through. I didn't plan to fall into a cavern. I thought I'd hike around for a while, then go back to school." He steepled his fingertips together. "But that's no excuse—I was stupid."

"But you *were* looking for something."

"Sure—petroglyphs. I certainly didn't expect to find any. I just hoped there'd be more locations—a pipe dream, you know?" Greg shook his head and exhaled. "I knew it was probable that all major sites were submerged when the dams were built. But I also wondered if every possible spot had been checked. You know how it is when an idea starts bugging you, just won't leave you alone." He tipped his head toward me with his eyebrows arched. "Don't you?"

"The bane of anthropologists." I shared his grin. "What made you pick that particular spot?"

"Last summer, when Mac took me fishing, we anchored near there. I saw the rock slide and wondered what had caused it. Maybe part of a lava shelf had given way, removing support from the shelf above. I wondered if that kind of thing had happened farther in—if the basalt from one flow was weaker than that formed by the next flow. I read about it in one of your books—about the potential for caves within layers. Thought it'd be fun to have a look."

"Fun." I chuckled, but stopped quickly and held my side. "Oooo." I bit my lip.

Lindsay leaned in and pecked Greg on the cheek. "You two have a lot to catch up on. I need to go open the museum. I'll see you later."

I raised my eyebrows at Greg after Lindsay left the room.

He shrugged, grinning even wider than before.

"We are going to talk about that—later. Petroglyphs first." I scooted to the edge of my chair.

Greg leaned forward. "Did you see them?"

"Yeah—amazing."

"I have to find out where he saw the originals."

"What do you mean—originals?"

"They're not real. I mean, they're real, but they're not authentic. Didn't you notice?"

"I was worried about you. You had a lot more time to check them out than I did." I wrinkled my nose. "How do you know?"

"They're all recent—really recent. I think one of the marijuana workers was bored, so he chipped those designs in the rock. With modern tools—a hammer and chisel, even—it wouldn't take as long as it used to. Clearly he practiced his technique and improved. The owl was his masterpiece."

"Back up." I flapped my hand. "I feel like Rip Van Winkle. Marijuana worker?"

"I don't know—he probably has a more technical job description. Didn't Sheriff Marge tell you? About the cavern being used as a marijuana depot?"

My eyes bulged.

"Oh. Well, the cavern has a river entrance, hidden well by scrub brush rooted in the mud bank. It's accessible with a shallow-bottomed boat. You and I entered the hard way. The cartel was using the cavern as a collection-and-distribution point—ferrying their goods on the river. Sheriff Marge thinks they cleared it out right after the grow on Julian's property was raided. They had a lot of dope to move in a hurry."

"So someone with the cartel made the petroglyphs?"

"Yeah, that's my guess. A watchman or something—he was probably bored and looking for a way to kill time. These guys aren't tourists. They don't go to interpretive centers or on the guided tours at state parks, so he wouldn't have seen the local petroglyph exhibits—either the replicas or the protected sites. He must have spotted actual petroglyphs while he was working on a grow, back in the hills somewhere around here." Greg's eyes were alight with excitement.

"But the carvings were higher on the walls than I can reach."

"Sheriff Marge said they had racking in the cavern, all around the periphery and in the center. There are marks from metal posts—heavy—the racks were holding a lot of weight. But if he climbed on top of the racks, he had, essentially, a clean slate to work on."

"Wow. How sure are you?"

"Pretty sure. It took me a couple days to work it out. Light filters in through the cavern entrance for a few hours in the afternoons. Lying there, I could see his progression. He was quite methodical."

"Now you're going to want to tag along with Sheriff Marge every time the deputies raid a grow."

"If she'll let me."

I laughed, then winced, again. "You have to write this up. It could turn into a whale of a thesis." I frowned. "Except I didn't do you any favors with Dr. Elroy."

"Lindsay told me about that. It explains quite a bit, actually."

"I mishandled the situation, I think. And I'm sorry about Angie—did Lindsay mention—?"

"She was very diplomatic." Greg nodded. "I'm not really that surprised. I knew Angie wasn't ready to settle down."

"Hence, Lorenzo." I shook my head. "But Lindsay's a sweetheart."

"I've figured that out." Greg's cheeks flushed.

"Right. Then I'll stop being nosy—for now. Have you talked to your mom?"

"Yeah."

"Is she coming?"

"No. She has a cruise to Mexico next week. Nonrefundable. I told her she should go."

"Greg, I'm sorry."

"Nah. Mom's not cut out to be a nurse." Greg smoothed the blanket across his good leg.

I was suddenly exhausted. "I better get back to my bed before I fall asleep again. When will you be mobile?"

"After they take these out." Greg raised his arm, which had familiar tubes stuck in it. "Can't operate crutches and drag an IV stand at the same time."

ooo

The doctor woke me up. He poked and prodded for a few minutes, looked in my nose and ears and down my throat, checked my temperature.

"Mm-hmm." He typed something into my chart. "You can go home tomorrow. You'll be sore for a while, and you have to wear the sling for at least six weeks."

"No surgery?"

"Right now the broken ends of your collarbone are slightly overlapped. If they heal that way, there might be a bump that bothers you later. It would be where a seat belt crosses over your shoulder, so it could be a nuisance. If we need to, we can do minor surgery later and shave the bump off. We'll look at it when you have X-rays in six weeks. We'll also talk about rehab after the X-rays." He took his glasses off and stuck them in his breast pocket. "I can give you a painkiller prescription if you want, but I'd prefer you use over-the-counter meds. Finish the ten-day antibiotic regimen for the sinus infection. And stay out of caves."

"Okay. I think I've had enough of prescription medications for a while."

"Good girl." His lab coat swished as he left.

An asymmetrical head in a knit cap popped into the doorway. "All clear?"

"Mac. Come in."

"Well, it's not just me." He made come-on gestures in the hall and ducked into my room.

Ford, panting, sprinted into my room, following a galloping Tuppence on a short leash.

"Hey," I squealed.

"Ssshhhh," Mac stage-whispered. "Animals aren't allowed. We're sneaking them in."

Tuppence climbed onto the bed and stuck her nose in my face.

I blocked the dog with my good arm. "Watch the ribs, okay, old girl? You smell like—like lemon." I wrinkled my nose. Lemon dish soap.

"We gave them baths," Ford said. "You have to be clean in a hospital."

I wondered if Ford had taken a bath, too. It didn't look like it.

Tuppence lay across my legs and settled her muzzle in the blankets. I rubbed her silky ears. What a sweet dog.

"This is the best, you guys. Thanks so much."

"There's more," Ford said. He unzipped his coveralls to midchest, revealing red thermal, long underwear and an orange fluff ball tucked inside.

"You found Tommy!"

"Sure is a friendly fellow. Eats a lot."

A muffled, squeaky purr started.

"Ford, he's a stray. He needs a good home. Why don't you adopt him?"

Ford's stumpy grin spread wide, and his eyes lit up. "Really?"

"Yes. It's obvious he likes you."

"Well, I can do that," Ford said, zipping up the coveralls and holding the sandwiched lump against his heart.

"I heard you're going home tom—" The previous day's nurse, in a fresh set of Tasmanian Devil cartoon scrubs, stopped short in the doorway. "Oh. You have visitors."

Mac snatched his cap off, and Ford stared. The effect of a pretty woman.

She stammered a little at the attention. "O-oh, a-and a dog."

Tuppence thumped her tail.

"I hope it's all right," I said.

"Just don't let the shift supervisor see. I won't tell."

Mac stuck out his hand. "Mac MacDougal, friend of Meredith's."

"Nancy Riley."

Mac held her hand too long, and Ford chortled, "Nurse Nancy."

"The patient's had a long day," Nancy said. "You can see her again tomorrow before she goes home. Is one of you giving her a ride?"

"Sheriff Marge'll want to do that," Mac said.

Nancy tugged on Tuppence's leash, and the dog hopped to the floor. "Quick. The hall's empty."

Ford waved, still grinning. Tommy purred incognito.

Nancy washed her hands and checked my IV bag. "The one in the coveralls, does he have a medical condition?" She pointed to her own chest. "The bulge—here?"

"Cat," I replied.

"Ah," Nancy said, but her look indicated she didn't fully comprehend. "Well, let's take out the IV, shall we?"

ooo

Julian arrived bearing a vase filled with daisies and bachelor's buttons. No one had brought me chocolate. Was it taboo these days—not healthy or something?

He pulled a chair up beside the bed. "How are you?"

"Okay. I'm going home tomorrow."

"I heard. Good." He rested his elbows on his knees and stared out the window.

"Hey," I said softly to bring his attention back. "How are *you*?"

He just shook his head, so I reached out my hand. He sort of had to take it. I squeezed.

"When's the service?"

"Saturday." His voice was weary, flat.

"Can I come?"

"Yeah. I'd like that. It'll be small. Esperanza—she's been our housekeeper since before Bard was born—the Levines, Marge, you."

"I think George would want to come. It might help him, too, you know, to . . . finish."

"You're right." Julian nodded. "I'll go see him tomorrow. I need to thank him."

"Yeah," I whispered.

CHAPTER 23

Sheriff Marge came in while a new nurse was showing me how to fit the sling on my right arm and across my left shoulder.

"Sheriff's chauffeur service," she announced.

I winced.

"Sorry," the nurse said. "It's tricky when you have cracked ribs, too. You're probably going to need help with this for the first few days until you get the hang of it."

"Or just not shower," I said.

"Huh-uh," Sheriff Marge grunted. "We'll work something out."

The nurse commandeered a cart and loaded all my flowers. She turned the cart over to Sheriff Marge so she could push me in the wheelchair.

"Hospital policy," she said when Sheriff Marge huffed.

We stopped by Greg's room and found Betty keeping him company. A vase of yellow carnations sat on his bedside table, but more than that—he had *three* boxes of chocolates. Why did he get all the good stuff?

"Are those for me?" Greg asked.

"Yes," I answered. "Sheriff Marge, would you?" I pointed to the shelf under the television. The nurse helped Sheriff Marge unload the cart.

"I was joking," Greg said.

"I'm not. I don't have room for all of these in my trailer. They're better where more people can enjoy them. Any idea how long you'll be here?"

"Another day or two at least."

"He's coming home with me when he's released," Betty said. "I had five children on a farm. I know all about caring for broken bones."

I smiled at Greg, and he smiled back. Betty was a far better mother than his real one.

"And I haven't forgotten you and Tuppence promised to come for a tour, Meredith," Betty said.

"When I can drive, we'll be there. And I promise to drive safely from now on," I said.

"Speaking of driving, Greg," Sheriff Marge interrupted, "the insurance adjuster was at the impound lot today, looking at your car. It's a total loss. They're figuring out how much to write the check for."

"I can't believe I forgot to set the parking brake."

"Could be it popped off. I've seen that happen before."

Greg sighed. "Well, it's done now." He turned to me. "I'll be back at the museum as soon as I can hobble around."

"And make a petroglyph info sheet so my deputies and I know what to look for when we're searching wilderness land for drugs or missing persons—or whatever." Sheriff Marge gave him the no-nonsense look over the tops of her glasses. "The Confederated Tribes are very interested in your hypothesis."

Greg was still beaming when we said good-bye.

I eased onto the bench seat in Sheriff Marge's Explorer. "Any chance you could drive below the speed limit and avoid all potholes?"

"If I get an emergency call, I have to go."

"I know," I grumbled. "I heard you're attending Bard's funeral Saturday. Could I beg another ride from you?"

"I was counting on it."

We rode in companionable silence until Sheriff Marge turned off the highway and pulled up in front of the courthouse.

"How are you holding up?" Sheriff Marge asked. "I have something to show you."

I unclenched my teeth. "I'm going to be uncomfortable no matter where I am, so yeah—I'm curious."

Sheriff Marge led me down to the chilly courthouse basement and into a room with no furniture and a big window.

The room smelled as though all the residual cigarette smoke from a bygone era had settled into the basement and rotted. There was also a hint of moldy linoleum and the chemical-powder scent of an air freshener—an exercise in futility.

Sheriff Marge pressed the buzzer on an intercom box and said, "Okay, Dale, bring 'em in."

The door to the room on the other side of the window opened, and a line of men walked in. The first wore slate-blue coveralls with his name embroidered on the chest in red cursive letters. Jerry. Some looked like they'd slept on a park bench the night before, others a little more presentable.

I realized I was looking through a one-way mirror. The next man to enter made the breath catch in my throat.

"Wait until they're all in," Sheriff Marge cautioned. "Then I want to know if you recognize any of them."

Dale's voice sounded eerie through the speaker. "Turn and face the mirror. Hold up your number."

The men did as instructed.

"Two and five," I said, still holding my breath. "They're the ones."

"Let's make this official," Sheriff Marge said. "The ones who what?"

"Who struggled with Bard at the end of the dock, who knocked him unconscious and tried to roll him into their boat but missed and rolled him into the river instead."

"Which one knocked Bard on the head?"

"Five."

"You sure?"

"Yes."

Sheriff Marge buzzed the intercom. "All right. We're finished."

The door in the other room opened, and the men filed out.

"I'm real glad you didn't pick number eight," Sheriff Marge said. "Jerry's our custodian. He fills in when we're short." She laughed. "We had to pull all the meth-heads and driving-while-suspendeds we could find just to get a reasonable lineup."

"But how did you find those two?"

"Henry was fooling around in one of his experimental choppers yesterday and spotted them on Graves Island. They'd had engine trouble, flooded it trying to get it restarted, then bent the shaft when they hit rocks near the island. At least that's what we think happened. They were cold and hungry, but they aren't talking. They're on ICE holds for now."

I shivered. "What about Bard?"

"When we retrieved their boat, we found a ten-pound, short-handled sledgehammer in the water below. They probably threw it overboard. There are traces of blood and hair in the boat, maybe from the hammer. The medical examiner's hurrying to compare the hammer to the indentation in Bard's skull so he can release the body for the funeral. He'll have DNA from the samples checked against Bard, too."

Sheriff Marge moved in front of me and held my gaze. "You also need to know the ME determined the injury to Bard's brain was sufficient to cause death. Bard would have died within a few minutes even if he hadn't been in the water, well before an ambulance could have arrived. The prosecuting attorney is going to charge number five with murder."

I blinked back tears.

"You couldn't have saved him, Meredith. There was nothing you could have done," Sheriff Marge said softly. "Okay?"

I nodded.

"I think he may have been killed as retribution for my raiding the grow. We all feel a measure of guilt in this." Sheriff Marge sighed and looked away. "I think at this point, Mort would say God's grace is sufficient. I'm counting on it—I have to." She took her glasses off and rubbed her eyes.

"What about the gash on Bard's forehead?"

"Postmortem, according to the ME. Probably hit a rock or submerged log while moving with the current." Sheriff Marge heaved a sigh and replaced her glasses. "I gotta make a call, then I'll take you home. Wait here."

I pressed my forehead against the cool mirrored glass and closed my eyes. My knees were trembling. My mind skipped back to that dark night and the horrible scene captured in the truck's headlights.

A life cut short. Julian would have gladly traded places with his son. Would I have traded places with Greg, if given the chance?

"Thank you," I whispered. "Thank you for a life spared." I thought for a minute. "Make that two lives—mine included."

CHAPTER 24

Sheriff Marge pulled up in front of my fifth-wheel, joining several other vehicles.

"What's going on?" I asked.

"Just a little welcome-home party."

I groaned.

"They won't stay long, but they were driving me crazy with offers to help. I had to suggest something for them to work on to keep them out of my hair. Come on."

Sheriff Marge bustled around and slammed the Explorer door shut after I eased myself to the ground. Tuppence greeted us and wriggled around our legs in glee.

"Mac drove your truck back, and he and Ford have been taking care of Tuppence and the cat."

"I know. They visited me in the hospital. All of them." I bent stiffly at the waist to stroke Tuppence's head.

Sheriff Marge chuckled. "And Rupert arrived late last night."

I stopped still. "I forgot."

"He's mighty glad his beloved employees are okay. And I think he brought you another surprise."

I grinned. "I'm not sure he can top the chamber pots." It would be good to see my boss. He'd be around for a couple months until wanderlust claimed him again.

Sheriff Marge opened the RV door and held it as I carefully climbed the steps. The trailer hummed with conversation and laughter. I poked my head through the doorway into a mass of warm bodies. Standing room only.

"Hey," Mort said. "There she is."

Mac, Ford, Mort and Sally, Lauren and Paul, Lindsay, Betty, Nadine—her bullet bra taking up space for two—and Rupert.

He looked good—tanned, so he hadn't spent his entire trip in Germany. I'd have to weasel out the details of his excursion. Maybe a couple more inches around the waist, too. Rupert always savors the local specialties, wherever he is. Think of a shorter, more rotund version of a sixty-year-old Sean Connery—that's Rupert. Minus the brogue, but just as roguish. He gives perma-set ladies the vapors, and I adore him for completely different reasons.

I sidled through painful jostling and patting as people tried to welcome me without bumping my sling. Rupert nearly crushed me anyway with a meaty bear hug that left me gasping.

"We'll catch up"—his deep, gravely voice tickled against my ear—"after you've taken a few days off. You should rest."

Sally and Lauren cornered me in the kitchen. Casserole dishes and Crock-Pots covered every square inch of counter space.

"We organized some food—" Sally began.

"And we thought it'd be a good chance to vet some of the recipes for the fundraiser cookbook," Lauren added. "I have evaluation forms here, so you can fill out one for each casserole. We're not telling who made what, so you can be completely unbiased."

"They're second- or third-hand recipes that have been submitted," Sally said. "Since we weren't familiar with them personally, we thought they should be tested. Everyone's so glad you and Greg are safe, and they wanted to contribute somehow." She looked around, hands on hips. "I'm afraid we may have overdone it a little."

"Is it all right if I share?" I asked.

"Of course."

I bit my lip. "You all are so good to me." To my surprise I teared up a little.

I got squeezed from both sides.

"Ooo—we're not supposed to do that. Are you okay?" Lauren asked.

"Yeah," I whispered. "I'll take hugs from friends any day."

Guests rotated through. Gloria from Junction General, Herb and Harriet, Dale—who must have rushed over from the courthouse—and his wife, Sandy, and several others from the football potlucks whom I recognized but didn't know by name. They departed quickly, as promised.

Only Mac and Ford remained when there was a knock on the door—Julian.

"I knew about the party, but—" he said. His face was lined and haggard, as though he had been going without sleep. "I saw George, and he sent along some smoked sturgeon for you." He handed me a neatly wrapped packet.

"Thanks. Come in. Your timing is perfect. You could relieve me of more casserole."

The faint smile reached his eyes. He held my gaze a few seconds.

"Mac, Ford." He acknowledged them with a nod of his Stetson.

"You guys look this stuff over and see what you want," I said. "I'm counting on you to take a lot."

Another knock. I opened the door.

Pete with an orchid. A really gorgeous orchid. Better than chocolate. And from Pete—hunky, irritating Pete. Pete, who, last time I'd seen him, held my hand. And in the cavern, he must have held even more. I wished I could remember that part in greater detail. I wished I could remember if I'd mumbled something stupid or brash or terribly forward in my delirium.

I realized my mouth was open. "Oh."

"Those other flowers won't last too long, so I brought you a plant."

"It's beautiful."

"Can I come in?"

"Yeah, oh, yeah, of course." I backed out of the way. "We're just divvying up the casseroles."

More nods and taciturn greetings. There was a whole lot of testosterone in my trailer. It felt stuffy.

"Have you decided what you want?" I tried to break the awkward tension.

The four men crowded around my kitchen island surveying the goods.

"I don't know about this broccoli thing," I said, scrutinizing a brownish-gray gelatinous slab dotted with moss-green florets. The puckered, drying surface was pulling away from the edges of the nine-by-thirteen pan. It looked like it had been made two weeks ago.

Mac leaned over my shoulder to check it out and shrank back.

"I'll take it," Pete said.

"You like broccoli?" I asked doubtfully.

"I can handle it." He gazed at me with steady blue eyes. The showdown at the O.K. Corral.

I flinched first. "Okay." I wouldn't mind him handling a few other things as well.

I replaced the foil cover while the men scooped mounds of scalloped potatoes embedded with jalapeño pepper slices, chicken rice pilaf, sweet-and-sour meatballs, turkey tetrazzini, spinach-stuffed cannelloni, and other dishes less identifiable into containers. Then they loaded plates from the dessert pans—brownies, jam bars, lemon bars, cherry strudel.

"Let me know your favorites. I have to report back to the cookbook committee."

I saw Mac, Ford, and Julian to the door, but Pete lingered.

"Need help cleaning up?"

I must have looked surprised.

"I do all my own cooking on the tug, you know."

"Thanks. I am a little limited since I'm not naturally left-handed. I will have trouble lifting heavy pans. Could you clear space in the fridge and cram everything in there?"

He worked efficiently, not at all flustered. I would have been jittery if our roles had been reversed. I was jittery anyway.

"Thanks for the orchid. It really is lovely."

"Sure," he said, into the fridge. "I'd like to see you again."

Kind of hard not to see me in a town this size. Was he asking for a date? "You do have to bring that pan back. I don't even know who it belongs to, so I'd hate to have it go missing on my watch."

His mouth didn't smile, but the corners of his eyes crinkled. "You may have to come get it, then."

I scowled.

"I'll let you know when I'm done with it."

He balanced the pan on his forearm and gazed at me from the other side of the island so long I thought I was going to melt. Either that or jump over the counter into his arms. Talk about jittery, but I couldn't tear my eyes away from his.

He let himself out, and I exhaled.

I collapsed onto the bed, my neck, shoulder, and ribs aching. The party had given me an unexpected shot of energy—now the crash. Then I got up to pop a couple of Tylenol, per doctor's orders, and nestled against the pillows for a long nap.

My stomach woke me up. I swallowed a few more Tylenol, then padded into the kitchen in the semidarkness and found the pan of brownies. Good enough. Not bothering to turn on any lights, I settled in the recliner with the pan on my lap and Tuppence's head on my foot and ate until I was almost sick—but not quite.

Brakes squealed to a stop outside. I scootched out of the chair and opened the door before Sheriff Marge knocked.

"Just checking on you. Sorry I had to leave before the party wound up. I hope they didn't stay too long?" Sheriff Marge puffed from her climb up the two steps.

"Not at all. Thanks for arranging everything."

"Gotta love these people. They pull you out of the side of a cliff so they can bury you in casseroles."

I chuckled. "I do. Love them."

"DEA just gave us our suspects' real names and confirmed they are Sinaloa cartel members. They want to comb the rest of Julian's land. They think there could be other marijuana grows out there."

"Right away?"

"I suggested they hold off until after the funeral, and they agreed." She scanned the kitchen. "You're all cleaned up. I was going to help you do that."

"Pete did it."

Sheriff Marge raised her eyebrows. "So he's useful in the kitchen, too?"

I grinned and shook my head. "And I had several volunteers to help eat the food."

"Oh, I was going to tell you—I noticed there was a broccoli and cream of mushroom soup dish. Write that one off. Absolute veto. I know whose that is, and it will make you sicker than a dog."

I stared at Sheriff Marge in horror, my jaw slack.

Sheriff Marge squinted. "What? Well, it could just be me, but if I were you, I'd be careful."

ooo

I napped between short walks with Tuppence the following day. Tylenol or Advil every four hours and lots of fresh air. I was getting the creaks out, building stamina, luxuriating in my new freedom. The worry about Greg—the overhanging helplessness and dread—had been a huge weight, its magnitude not fully realized until it was gone. I talked on the phone with both Greg and Rupert several times.

Sheriff Marge picked me up on Saturday morning for the drive to Julian's ranch. I scanned the port dock by the grain elevators and the marina as we sped past, looking for Pete's tug, but it wasn't there. Did I owe him an apology for a bout of food poisoning?

Sheriff Marge reached across me and popped open the glove compartment.

"Those are yours," she said, pointing at a wadded plastic grocery bag stuffed on top of the papers and ice scraper.

I pulled the bag out and opened it. Magnets with ladies' names on them.

I started in surprise. "You caught him? You've been busy."

Sheriff Marge chuckled. "Didn't catch him, just picked him up. The clerk at the hardware-and-pharmacy place in Lupine recognized him and held him till we could get there. Matched your description exactly except he's now suffering from a terrible head cold. Swore he was only there to buy decongestant."

Sheriff Marge succumbed to a high, wheezy laugh that I'd never heard before, and a tear leaked out of the corner of her eye. She swiped at it.

"I've seen a lot over the years, but the funniest thing I might have ever seen was when his grandmother came to the jail—little bitty thing in shawls and curlers—and stuck her hand through the bars to get her teeth back so she could chew him out." She howled and slapped the steering wheel. "Apparently there aren't enough teeth to go around in that family, and he borrowed hers when he went to town."

Sheriff Marge reveled in the memory for several minutes, then sighed. "Just when you're sure there's nothing new under the sun, something like that comes out of the blue." She shook her head. "The money and the tape dispenser are gone. It's unclear what happened to the tape dispenser, and I didn't press the issue. Do you care about the money?"

"Nope."

"Good. It probably fed his family for a week. His grandmother said she thought he had a job, thought that's how he was bringing home the groceries. He lives with her plus four younger half siblings. I got them set up with social services."

"What about the shotgun?"

"He didn't have it when we arrested him, and he said the gun wasn't loaded when he threatened you. Granny brought it in the next day, wrapped in a burlap sack. Just left it on Nadine's desk without a word."

Sheriff Marge drove for what seemed like miles up Julian's graded and graveled driveway, past a sprawling ranch house and several machine sheds.

I spotted Jesus Hernandez working on a tractor. So Julian had given him work for the winter.

The Explorer rumbled over washboard tire tracks along a rusted barbed wire fence to a hillock overlooking the river. Short crosses and a few headstones stood among the waving grass in silhouette against the wan powder-blue sky.

"It's a family plot," Sheriff Marge said. "Several generations of Josephs are buried here. I was last here for Lizzie's funeral." She sighed heavily, opened the door, and swung her short legs to the ground.

We climbed the slight rise and joined a small group standing beside the rectangular hole Julian had ready. The coffin was in place at the bottom. An extra-long pine box.

Mort and Sally sang a hymn. A small dark-haired woman stood next to me, sniffling into a handkerchief—Esperanza, the housekeeper.

Julian kept his head bent, face hidden behind the Stetson's brim.

Mort said some things about the Good Shepherd and about life being like the grass of the field and a puff of wind. He didn't linger.

He picked up three shovels and handed one each to Julian and George. They worked fast and hard until their skin glistened with sweat, to cover the boy who had come home to stay.

Esperanza laid a bunch of sunflowers on the mound.

A few murmurs, a handshake, an arm around the shoulders. There wasn't much to say. I held Julian's hand until he nodded at me. The golden eyes were brighter today. He would survive.

George was by my side as we walked back to the parked cars. He looked straight ahead when he spoke, into the wind and the blowing grass. "Come for tea when you're ready."

I smiled. "I will."

SNEAK PEEK

DOUBLED UP

An Imogene Museum Mystery
Book 2

Meredith Morehouse, curator of the eclectic Imogene Museum, stumbles upon the remnants of a stolen shipment of scary-looking wood figurines. Are they smuggled national treasures or clever fakes?

While Meredith is sucked into the secret federal probe of the fishy figurines and their importer, her ex-fiancé—a man so annoyingly arrogant he could easily drive someone to murder—returns for another round of marriage proposals, and he won't take no for an answer. Just when her friendship with hunky tug boat captain Pete Sills might be heating up.

What's a girl to do?

1

The windshield wipers couldn't keep up. They squeaked rapid arcs across the glass, but my view of the highway wavered into watery columns regardless. The entire Columbia Gorge had been blanketed by a low-pressure soaker for the past four days, long enough that even the earthworms were coming up for air and drowning on the pavement. I had tried to tiptoe around the bloated white squiggles while splashing the short distance from my fifth-wheel trailer to the pickup, but I was pretty sure gummy residue coated the thick soles of my hiking boots anyway.

Fashion went out the window on days like this. Silk long underwear, flannel-lined jeans, thick wool socks, a thermal T-shirt, and a bulky cabled sweater puffed me up like the Michelin Man under a bright-yellow hooded raincoat. But I was warm and dry.

I turned off the highway into the access road for my place of employment, the Imogene Museum. We'd be lucky to get any visitors today. The Columbia River Gorge isn't scenic when the bellies of dark rain clouds float just feet off the choppy gray water and hide the forested hills on either side.

I relish the solitude, actually—a rare chance to do the important, and usually neglected, curator's task of entering more of the museum's collection of random oddities into the database tracking system.

The mansion that houses the museum is by no means silent or lonely, even when empty. The old girl (built in 1902) creaks and clanks, whistles and groans, like a decommissioned frigate straining against her final anchor chain, waiting for the blast that will send her to the bottom. Sometimes I talk back, promising the trustee board will keep patching her up as best they can.

The previous day's puddles had amassed into mini lakes splotching the muddy lawn. I picked out Ford Huckle's cabin through the spindly arms of bare oaks and maples. He lives in a converted pump house, one of the many outbuildings on the museum's sprawling acreage. I hoped the groundskeeper's new septic system could handle the rising water table. A bright-blue Honey Bucket porta-potty still stood next to the cabin's front door, providing a shot of startling color in the otherwise drab landscape.

I turned into the paved parking lot shared by the museum, county park, and marina. A semitruck idled longways directly in front of the museum, blocking the entrance sidewalk. A blackish exhaust cloud hugged the asphalt, unable to rise through the downpour.

The white trailer was unmarked, but the passenger-side door of the dark-green cab said "T&T Trucking, Seattle, WA." Probably a long-haul driver who'd pulled off the highway last night when the rain was so hard he couldn't see. Plus, there are rules about the maximum number of hours a driver can be on the road in any twenty-four-hour period, in order to prevent sleepy drivers from becoming a safety hazard. He'd probably left the engine running to keep the cab heated while he dozed.

As I slowed to a stop, I realized the driver must be in the trailer, because the rear door was rolled up. A few pieces of broken wood pallet littered the ground outside the trailer.

I slid my right arm back into the sling that was supposed to keep my shoulder and broken collarbone immobilized, and hopped out of the pickup, pulling my hood up to shield my face from the pelting rain. The empty right sleeve of my raincoat flapped as I trotted around to the back of the trailer and peered inside.

"Hello?" I called.

Splintered wood, broken crates, clumps of raffia-like packing material, and wads of plastic wrap were strewn on the trailer's floor. Scuff marks disturbed what appeared to be sawdust.

I couldn't see all the way to the front end, but it did look as though there were more boxes and crates farther in. Some of them might still be intact. Who would unload crates in the museum's parking lot in the middle of the night?

Unless Rupert had yet another surprise up his sleeve. I grinned.

Rupert Hagg is the museum director and great-grandnephew of the mansion's builder, the philanthropist and visionary Wilder Hagg. Rupert had inherited responsibility for the nonprofit museum. He'd hired me to do the day-to-day organizing and managing while he traveled the globe looking for items to add to the museum's roster. Maybe Rupert was in the museum, unpacking goodies.

I dashed toward the museum's front doors, but skidded to a stop after just a few steps. In my peripheral vision, a rotund, person-shaped lump lay on the ground beside the back wheels of the truck cab. Yes. He'd been hidden from view when I was on the other side of the trailer.

The driver's door was open. Had he fallen out?

I gulped, trying to remember the basics of CPR from the lifeguarding class I took in high school a couple of decades ago.

I ran back and knelt beside the man. He looked as white and bloated as the worms I'd stepped on earlier. I jabbed two fingers in the fleshy fold between his jaw and neck. Maybe a little blip, blip, blip of a pulse. Maybe it was my imagination.

I leaned over, my cheek skimming his nose. Ragged, raspy breathing and a bitter, acrid smell. His salt-and-pepper mustache was stained tobacco-brown directly under his nostrils.

I picked up a plump hand that was surprisingly soft but heavy and limp. His steel-gray button-down uniform shirt said "Terry" on the pocket that bulged around a pack of cigarettes. Presumably one of the *Ts* of T&T Trucking. I rubbed his hand but didn't get a response. Still, his chest rose and fell in a regular cadence, and I was glad his life didn't depend on my shaky memory of CPR.

He was soaked to the skin. How long had he been lying here? In this rain, it wouldn't have taken long to get that wet.

I sprinted to my pickup to fish my cell phone out of my tote and grab the hairy old blanket Tuppence, my hound, sat on when she rode shotgun. I grunted as I tried to manage everything one-handed, still feeling twinges of unexpected pain with certain movements. With the blanket wedged under my right arm, I palmed the phone and ran back to the unconscious driver.

I flung the blanket over him, pulling and nudging to get most of him covered. Calling Sheriff Marge Stettler guaranteed as quick a response as calling 911, and sometimes a quicker one. Sheriff Marge was always on duty.

"Unconscious truck driver in the museum parking lot," was all I had to say.

"It'll have to be the volunteer fire department," Sheriff Marge replied. "The EMTs are in a training session at the hospital in Lupine. Get him warm and dry."

"I'm trying," I said to dead air.

He was lying in about half an inch of water. I pulled off my raincoat and spread it over him. He was too heavy to drag one-armed, and until we knew what had caused his condition, he probably shouldn't be moved.

I climbed the steps to the cab, hanging on with my left hand, and fell stomach-first onto the driver's seat. Maybe he'd have something I could use.

I scooted around until I was sitting behind the wheel. The cab was littered with crumpled potato chip bags, empty plastic drink bottles, and fruit pie wrappers. A bobblehead Chihuahua clung to the dashboard by a grimy suction cup. It jiggled above a protruding ashtray that overflowed with putrid butts.

No umbrella, tarp, rain poncho—nothing water-resistant. I reached through the steering wheel with my left hand and rocked the key in the ignition until the rumbling engine shut down.

My foot bumped something light on the floor, and I bent to look. An inflated doughnut seat cushion, the kind new mothers sit on. And truck drivers, apparently. I tossed the cushion out the open door and eased down the steps.

Kneeling above the driver's head, I slipped my right arm out of the sling and used both hands to lift his head. I grimaced against the pain in my right shoulder and kneed the cushion underneath. He moaned. My hands came away bloody.

NOTES

The Imogene Museum mystery series is a tribute to the Columbia River Gorge and the hearty people who live in gorge towns on both sides of the Oregon/Washington border. It's an extraordinary piece of God's real estate, and I savor driving, sight-seeing, picnicking, and camping along its entire length. Hitching a ride on a tug run from Umatilla to Astoria is on my bucket list.

If you're familiar with the area, you may realize that I've taken liberties with distances in some cases. Mostly I squished locations (albeit fictional) closer together to move the story along and also to showcase the amazing geologic and topographic features of the gorge. In real life for many gorge residents, the round trip to a Costco or a bona fide sit-down restaurant might well take a full day. This kind of travel time is not helpful when you're chasing a fleeing murderer. But if you're not Sheriff Marge and have time to enjoy the scenery, the gorge is spectacular, and I encourage you to come experience it for yourself.

However, please don't expect to actually meet any of the characters in this book. All are purely fictional, and if you think they might represent anyone you know, you're mistaken. Really. I couldn't get away with that.

ACKNOWLEDGMENTS

Profound thanks to the following people who gave their time and expertise to assist in the writing of this book:

The wise, good-humored, and eagle-eyed ladies in my writing critique group—Diane Cammer, Sandy Stark, Anne Taylor, and Karen Williams.

My insightful beta readers—Debra Biaggi and BJ Thompson.

Detective Kevin Schmidt of the Clark County Sheriff's Office, who answered questions about guns, search and rescue, and evidence collection.

Sergeant Fred Neiman Sr. and all the instructors of the Clark County Sheriff's Citizen's Academy. The highlights had to be firing the Thompson submachine gun and stepping into the medical examiner's walk-in cooler. Oh, and the K-9 demonstration and the officer survival/lethal force decision-making test. And the drug task-force presentation with identification color spectrum pictures and the—you get the idea.

I claim all errors, whether accidental or intentional, solely as my own.

